LOKI'S GAME

LOKI'S GAME

Siobhan Kinkade

Phoenix & Fae Publications
Chester, South Carolina

Dedicated with love to my husband,
who puts up with more insanity on a daily basis
than most men do in their entire lives.

PROLOGUE

Thousands of years ago…

Fafnir looked down at his only child, and with a wet, rasping breath the dying dragon uttered the words, "Find the ring."

Little more than a whelp, sixteen-year-old Kenna wiped the tears from her eyes. As the battered old dragon returned to human form, she pressed a kiss to his forehead while he took his last breath. Her human mother also lay broken, used bait left on the floor of the cave where the trap had been set. Alone, she was now tasked with her family's burden.

"Yes, Father," she said to the dead man, and rose to her feet. Leading away from the cave — the only home she had ever known — was a trail of gold coins and bloody jewels. The dead dragon's blood smeared a thin, black trail where the horrid, heart-piercing weapon, Gram, slid along behind its owner. The Great Hero was wounded and obviously not aware of her presence or he likely would have taken much more care in covering his tracks.

Kenna's shifter senses picked up the scent of Sigurd's blood and her instincts took over. His soul was already tainted by the power of the ring and the taste of dragon's blood left on his fingers; she sensed evil flowing in his veins, warring with the inherent goodness of his station. This man, an unintentional pawn in the gods' selfish game, had come to retrieve a treasure with the purest of intent… Too bad he was too weak to fight the power he now held.

Should she not stop him, he would be back to take her father's heart and roast it over a fire. The birds told her many things, and had she been faster to return to her family's nest with her news, Fafnir's life might have been spared and in its place given his brother's. Regin deserved nothing less than death for his actions.

No doubt Regin's hand had been forced by that devious monster, Loki. Her father had warned her that he might want the treasure back. If he chose to take it he would stop at nothing to see that ring back in his hands for the power it held. She had never believed in such foolish stories. Kenna did not doubt the existence of the old gods, but she had never seen one, and aside from the powers bestowed upon her by Fafnir and his bloodline, she refused to let the story scare her.

Until now.

Removing her clothing, Kenna knelt close to the ground and allowed necessity to lead her change.

When it was complete, she viewed the world through the eyes of a wolf, and the essence of her father's attacker hung in the air like a cloud, dancing over the dropped gems like tiny beacon lights to lead her on her path.

Throwing her head back, the wolf-girl howled and leapt out into the night to hunt the dragon slayer and take back those things which had been stolen from her.

CHAPTER ONE

Rowan Keir paced the floor like a caged animal. Lately he spent more time than could possibly be healthy feeling trapped and restless. The last time he was this on edge all hell had broken loose and sent him on the run, hiding like a coward from an old enemy with a never-ending arsenal of tricks. But he had given Loki the slip four decades ago and had remained as low-profile as possible for just that reason.

Rowan liked Savannah and he liked the people there. Unfortunately, his nature did not easily lend itself to life as a wealthy recluse. He wanted to be out among people, to socialize and to see the sights. To embrace life even though he had a duty to fulfill—one passed down to him through the generations and through his blood. As the only child of now deceased parents, he was the last protector; the sole keeper of ancient secrets and an even older bloodline.

His life had been a lonely one since the appearance of Loki. Before the revelation that the old gods were real, he'd spent quite a bit of time in the company of others. The flashy lifestyle could certainly have played a role in his being found, but now to completely abandon himself—his dreams, his desires, his very *life*?

Absurd.

It was far past time for him to rectify the situation. Frustrated to the point of fury, Rowan crossed the room and pulled open the door.

"Dane!" he called down the hallway. A tall, blond man appeared, his hair slicked back against his head and gathered in a ponytail at the base of his neck. An intelligent, amber gaze met Rowan's, but the younger man said nothing as he quietly awaited his orders. Even at odd hours, Rowan could never remember seeing Dane anything less than perfectly presented. Certainly older than he appeared, Dane wore an agelessness in his sharp, angular features. Who or what he might be, Rowan had never dared to ask. It didn't matter to him.

While there was an odd camaraderie between them—Dane had been in his employ for the past twenty or so years—yet Rowan couldn't necessarily call him a friend. They had an unspoken understanding of one another which came with a level of almost familial affection, even if he was on payroll. "I need you to run an advertisement in the newspaper, as soon as possible."

"For what position?" the young man asked, raising a questioning eyebrow at his boss.

Odd behavior? Definitely. But isn't odd behavior what wealthy eccentrics are known for?

"I need..." Rowan faltered. Dane continued to watch him with the even, unmoving expression eternal patience. The man never lost his temper, and for a brief moment, Rowan felt the overwhelming urge to ruffle his feathers. Just for a moment...but then thought better of it. If not for Dane, he would be completely alone. Rowan sighed. "I have no idea what I need."

"A new employee?"

"Are you going somewhere?" The thought of losing Dane frightened him as little else could. The question brought a hint of a smile to his employee's lips.

"Wasn't planning on it."

"Good."

"Then perhaps a girlfriend?" Dane offered, and Rowan scoffed. Yet...a girlfriend might be exactly what he needed to work off some of this nervous energy. Hadn't he just been telling himself that he needed to get out more? Rowan realized even as he followed that thought down the rabbit hole that he was still pacing and forced himself to stand still.

"A girlfriend would help," he admitted, albeit grudgingly.

"Advertising for one might not be the best way to go about gaining female companionship," Dane said, his tone cautious. "The caliber of woman you

7

might encounter would be less than appropriate for someone of your stature." Of course she would, Rowan knew, but he could be considered an eligible bachelor, particularly with his money. There was no doubt in his mind the Savannah social scene would advertise him like he was the next big rock star.

Exactly the trouble with money.

He couldn't have that. Couldn't return to that high-profile lifestyle. Despite his whereabouts once again being unknown to the trickster, and thanks to Dane for making sure his tracks stayed covered, there was still too much of a chance Loki would find him that way. And Loki finding him would mean having to give up on whatever relationship he might be able to cultivate from the mess that was his life. Rowan had a very specific duty to uphold, a solemn vow to his dying father. And he hated it.

"I understand," Rowan said, and met Dane's questioning gaze. "But how else am I supposed to find a mate?"

"You could go out into the world and meet women like the rest of us."

No, that wouldn't do either. Too much chance for error. "I need advertisement, but I refuse to lie."

"Always the noble beast." The thin smirk at the corner of Dane's lips made Rowan want to smack the hell out of him. Snide little bastard.

"It is a requirement, you know."

"If you do not mind me saying so, your father, grandmother, and great-grandfather were all foolish. They looked for trouble when they went looking for Loki."

"No, they were determined to end the war." Rowan sighed. "I am a coward." He hated himself for admitting it, yet the truth would haunt him regardless of his acceptance. To outrun a god would be godlike in itself, and he could not be farther from such.

"You are very mistaken, sir."

"I do not believe you."

Dane nodded, and wiped the smug look from his face. "Say I were to help you with this fool's errand, what exactly would you be looking for?"

"A female—"

"I quite hope so."

"Smart ass."

"I try." Banter… That was new. Rowan mused over it as he continued with his list of requirements.

"Late twenties or early thirties. Intelligent. And someone who can easily deal with my…affliction."

Dane raised one well-trimmed eyebrow at Rowan, and his left cheek sucked in as if he were chewing it. Rowan deserved to be laughed at for this—it was the single-most inane idea he had ever had. Even in the whole of his six-hundred-plus years on earth.

"Wanted: single female, twenty-five to thirty-two?"

"Yes," Rowan replied with a sigh.

9

"A bit fatalistic if you ask me."

"Precisely why I didn't ask you," Rowan snorted. "If I am going to do this at all, I may as well invite every woman that fits the bill to apply."

Dane nodded and started down the stairs, only to pause and look back up. "Forgive me for being so blunt, but this is quite possibly the stupidest idea you have ever had."

"Yes," Rowan said and sighed as he pushed the door closed. "I know it is."

Savannah was not a huge city, but the population was large enough for relative obscurity unless one happened to be a debutante. That those existed at all still confused Rowan, but then again many of his sensibilities bordered on the archaic.

A caveman among aristocrats, Dane had called him on the first morning the advertisement ran. A fitting description, however annoyed Rowan might have been with it.

What·surprised him even more than the number of debutante balls held in a single year in Savannah was the sheer number of women who responded to his advertisement. For days, Dane spent hours poring over the letters of interest, the résumés, and the personal visits of women seeking any sort of employment, even the most vague kind.

Rowan tried his hardest to feel guilty about the promise of a job that did not exist, but with each passing day his restlessness grew. The walls seemed to close in on him just a little bit more. And though he knew he was living in relative obscurity, he retained that horrible feeling of being watched.

He had to find an outlet for the excess energy that even two-hour runs through swampland could not release, and history had taught him that nothing left a man pleasantly tired faster than a few rounds with an energetic woman. The more he thought about it, the more he craved physical human contact.

And with over two hundred résumés and personal applications to choose from, he was certain at least one of them would hit the mark. Rowan also counted himself lucky in that he had Dane to help weed out some of the less desirable applicants. Poor grammar and spelling were no contest—whatever woman Rowan chose to associate with needed a firm grasp on her language.

After nearly a week of constant reading of personal documents, Dane appeared before Rowan, slamming his palm down against the stack of papers. This was highly unusual—he never spoke out of turn, never acted out in such a way.

"Get out."

"Excuse me?" Rowan asked, startled by the demand.

"Leave this office," Dane said, his new tone of authority surprising. "Get out of the house. Go outside and interact with other people."

"Where is the fun in that?"

"Just do it."

Rowan sighed and scrubbed his hands through his hair, ruffling the papers on his desk. "I don't see the need."

"Because you are going stir crazy and I am tired of listening to you grunt and groan. Leave the building and don't come back for at least three hours." A new fire burned in the blond man's features, but he remained still as stone. "Go shopping. Go have dinner. Go anywhere. Just go. Now."

Dane wasn't going to back down on this one. Rowan reluctantly rose from his chair, tucked his feet into his shoes, and took the keys his assistant offered him. It would do no good to argue with the pigheaded young man, so rather than waste time, Rowan rose from the chair and started into the labyrinth of hallways that was his house toward the garage.

When he really thought about it, he realized he was a bit hungry.

As he opened the car door, he still found himself distracted by the task at hand. If only he could make this work, life would be much less unbearable. But then again, if he did manage to make it work, he might have to leave her behind should Loki come looking for him again. No matter his own personal desires, keeping Loki in the dark was his first priority.

Rowan shifted the expensive sports car into gear and tore out of the garage, leaving long streaks of black rubber on the fresh-paved street.

‹HAPTER TWO›

"I'm here to answer the ad in the paper."

Behind the desk, the well-dressed blond gentleman scarcely acknowledged her presence. He took her resume, looking disinterested. "Appointment?" he snapped, his tone more efficient than rude.

"Lily Redway."

"Have a seat."

She did, perching on the edge of the single, stiff chair. The room held only the desk, the receptionist, and this one chair. Panic shot through her, and for a moment she was certain she'd made a mistake in coming here. Any number of things could be happening behind that door across the way. This guy could easily be a serial killer; maybe they were chopping up women and selling their organs on the black market. Maybe the ad was vague for a reason.

Wanted: single female, 25-32.

The only other information had been a telephone number and this address. A residence, she'd realized with a bolt of fear. On a whim she had called, only to receive information as vague as and more confusing than what she already knew. Today's date and a time. "It will all be explained at your meeting," she'd been told when she questioned the job's duties, and the call disconnected. She assumed it was the same man that now sat across from her, doing his best to ignore her. The voices were very similar.

All of that and half a tank of gas to get across town in rush-hour traffic led her to this moment and the breath of paralytic fear as the door opened. Lurch at the desk pointed to it. She swallowed and smoothed her hand across the top of her head, checking for lumps in her hair. Her fingers brushed the still-tight chopsticks holding the dark chignon in place and she rose from the chair. If it weren't for her complete lack of a job, Lily would have gone running out the front door. Rather than give into her fear, she picked up her courage and crawled deeper into the old mansion, her kitten-heeled sandals clicking on the expensive tile under her feet.

Behind the door she found a long hallway which exited into a cozy sitting room. It had high ceilings with two large, overstuffed chairs that faced each other. Between the chairs sat a coffee table containing a steaming teapot, two cups, and a jar of honey. A fire crackled happily in the stone fireplace along the back wall, adding ambience to the soft glow of two floor lamps. Paintings hung on the walls; works which, if they were as originals they appeared to be, should have been in a gallery.

The house smelled of old wood and furniture polish despite the gentle lighting and freshly-renovated look. She'd always wanted to get into one of these houses and look around, but she never expected that pipe dream to manifest. Despite the vagueness of the ad and the inherent fear of a lurking madman, she appreciated the snooping opportunity it afforded her.

Even if it was the most unprofessional setting she had ever seen. It felt more like British High Tea than a job interview. But at the same time, these rich kooks liked to do strange things such as this in order to test their would-be employees. Looking around at all of the little personality quirks of the room, Lily assumed she was to sit, but in which chair? Perhaps that was the test.

She opted instead to stand, meandering to the fireplace to look at the painting above it. It was a Monet, and from the look of the brushstrokes, an original. The owner had to be beyond rich to afford something like that.

What have I gotten myself into? she wondered as yet another door opened. In walked a tall, broad-shouldered man. His blond hair, while brushed and perfectly neat, hung just beyond his shoulders in soft waves. A set of full, rose-colored lips rested amid pale stubble the same color of his hair. Those sinful lips broke into a broad smile that touched his eyes, making them sparkle. They were the color of the sky, flecked with gold and surrounded by a thick fringe of long lashes most women would kill for. He looked to be in his mid-thirties, but carried himself as if he were much, much older. Just the sight of him set her blood boiling in her veins.

"Good afternoon, Miss Redway," he said. She picked up a slight accent, but from where she couldn't be sure. "Please," he gestured to the chairs with a broad sweep of his arm, "have a seat." Lily hedged, forcing a smile to her lips. He stood by, patiently waiting, and she looked him over as she closed the space.

Definitely a test.

He wore a well-tailored suit with a long-waist coat of dark blue linen lined with black satin, and he moved like a man used to partaking of the finer things in life. His quiet confidence both excited and unnerved her. Lily perched on the edge of the chair, eyes still fixed on him. His smile was natural and easy, and put her on edge as he took the seat opposite her, sinking into its comfort as if he'd sat there a thousand times.

"Relax," he said. "Would you care for a cup of tea?"

"Thank you, Mr…"

"Rowan," he said, extending his hand toward her. "Rowan Keir." She accepted the friendly offer, prepared to shake it. Instead, he brought her hand to his lips and kissed the skin just behind her knuckles. "Enchantée." Lily cleared her throat to hide the girlish giggle threatening to escape. It was such a cheesy line, but so, so flattering.

"A pleasure, Mr. Keir."

"Call me Rowan."

"All right, Rowan," she said, trying hard to ignore the tingle across the back of her hand where his lips touched. "I don't mean to seem ungrateful, but I was hoping you could tell me what sort of job it is I'm applying for." He hit her with the full force of his smile, a sight that would have made her knees weak had she been standing.

"Very straightforward. I like that." He poured two cups of tea. "The position I offer is unique. It requires certain…talents." She swore his words had a double meaning as he pushed a cup toward her. "Honey?"

Lily had to clear her throat twice before speaking. "Thank you."

"This position will require close collaboration with me on many topics," he said blithely, as if he had not noticed the immediate effect he'd had on her. Lily knew men weren't immune to that sort of thing—he could probably smell the change in her body's chemistry…if not see the bright burn of embarrassment heating her cheeks.

"So, an assistant."

He smirked, and she went gooey inside. "Something like that."

At a complete loss for words, Lily lifted the cup to her lips. He watched her, mimicking her movements. Her eyes wandered back to the Monet painting above the fireplace, grasping for a way to break the tension. This man was not ordinary in any way, a realization both terrifying and refreshing. At least he would be anything but dull.

"Tell me a bit about yourself," Rowan said, startling her back to attention. His gaze was intense and intimate, and Lily cleared her throat nervously, hugging the teacup to her.

"I'm twenty-seven, never married, no pets, no job, and bills coming out of my ears." She took a sip of her tea. "Other than that, there isn't much to tell."

"That is unfortunate," Rowan said. The look on his face was strange, as if he didn't know how to verbalize the thoughts in his head.

"What about you?" Perhaps if she prompted him...

"Also not much to tell. Thirty-four. Never married. But I do have a pet." Lily barked a nervous giggle and they fell back into tense silence. She sipped her tea once more. Rowan looked around, admiring his collection.

Look at me like that, Lily caught herself thinking, and immediately squashed the thought. *Tension!* She couldn't stand it.

"The Monet...is that an original?" she asked. The question obviously pleased him.

"It is. An early variation of Water Lilies."

"So you're a collector?"

Rowan nodded. "You are an art lover," he replied. She blushed again, and felt silly for doing so.

"Sort of," she admitted. "I was an art history major. My specialization is Renaissance artwork." Why was she telling him this? He had her résumé!

"Impressive," he said as if he was just learning this information. "So far you are the only prospect who has been able to correctly name one of my paintings."

"Score one for the home team," she said, twirling one finger in a sarcastic fashion while attempting to ignore his comment—if he had more than one painting then she was in way over her head. He chuckled, and the sound shot through her like a surge of pure energy.

"And a sense of humor. Miss Redway, you are by far the most interesting woman I have met in years." She wasn't sure if that was a good thing. But one thing was certain…spending much more time in his presence would lead to very bad things. He was intoxicating, like a glass of fine, aged wine. Just this small taste of him already had her wanting more.

Stop it, she berated herself, *this is your future boss!* In one gulp, she drained her cup. Here she was already placing herself in the job, and she didn't even know what it was yet. This whole interview felt completely absurd—like it was only a front for something different. The longer she sat there, the less she felt like a job candidate and the more she felt like she was about to be propositioned. And she could not guarantee to herself that she would turn him down if he did.

Talk about skewed perceptions.

"So you know artwork," he continued with a smile. "What can you tell me of mythology?"

Lily shrugged. "Not much," she said, thankful for the abrupt change to a less personal subject. "I had to study the history around the time period relevant to my degree, but the ancient mythologies I can't say I know much about." Setting her cup on the table, she brushed a hand over the side of her head to make sure her hair was still in place. "I know the Greek and Roman stories from high school, but I don't really know much of the others." She pinned him with a steady gaze. "Is there a reason you ask?"

He smiled.

"I find myself drawn to the old histories," Rowan said. "Nordic mythology seems to be a particular favorite of mine."

"You mean Odin and Loki?"

"The very ones," he replied, and her heart leapt into her throat. She didn't know these things! She was losing her chance… She had to find a way to save this.

"Is that knowledge relevant to this job?" Lily asked.

"Not necessarily," he answered, and she relaxed a bit, watching him as he spoke and taking in the way his Adam's apple moved in speech, the way his lips formed around the words, and wondered for a moment what those lips would feel like forming around hers. "But I cannot promise that I will not bore you to tears with the stories."

"I like stories," she said dumbly. Lily grimaced and covered her face with her hand. She was making an absolute fool of herself, and all he could do was smile at her with his too-full lips and his bright, white teeth.

"More tea?" he asked, already pouring before she could answer. "So tell me something," he continued in an obvious attempt to put her mind at ease, "what made you answer such a vague advertisement?"

"Curiosity," she replied with a noncommittal shrug. "Masochism," she added and she heard his cup rattle on its saucer as he held in his laughter. "But mostly desperation. I *really* need a job."

"Again, points for honesty."

"Can I ask you a question?"

"Of course." An enigmatic smile played across his lips and his eyes glimmered with something wicked. Her throat went dry.

"Why would you post such a vague ad?"

"Those are the requirements."

"But I still have no idea what the job is!"

The good humor never left his eyes. "Consider it an engagement." He placed his cup to the side and rose. "Come, walk with me and I will try to help you understand."

She boggled at him, but did as he asked. Rowan extended his elbow and she slipped her hand through, and the urge to giggle swept over her again. Even beneath the fabric of his coat, his skin burned against her fingers. "Your résumé says you were a curator," he said, leading her through the door. "What happened?"

"The museum lost its funding and closed." She sighed. "The collection was scattered amongst the investors and returned to owners." Lily shrugged one shoulder, trying to hide her disappointment. "There isn't much call for an art history major anywhere else."

A low, vibrating chuckle escaped him, shimmering through her and all the way to the tips of her toes. Every cell in her body grew hotly aware of him, of his side brushing against the back of her hand as they walked.

"Your professors trained you well." Lily grinned at the compliment, and covered the motion with her hand. She didn't want to appear too eager or too smitten. Besides, in her experience, compliments were usually followed by less pleasant things. "Now what of your family?" he asked. Shaking the butterflies from her stomach, she dared a glance up at him. His profile wasn't one that could be considered perfect, but it was still enough to make her want to get closer — to completely derail her brain.

"My parents live in Tampa," she said. "I was already in Atlanta, so they left Charleston when my dad retired. I'm an only child."

"I am sorry to hear that. Being an only child can be lonely."

"'You know this from experience?"

"I do."

"What of your parents?" she asked.

"Deceased."

"I'm sorry."

"Do not be," he said, and laid a hand over her fingers, still curled at the crook of his elbow. The contact sizzled. "They lived long, full lives and wherever they are, I know they are together." They entered a room that she realized a moment too late was an elevator...not that it mattered. She wasn't the type to be interested in intimate contact against the wall of a moving elevator. At least, she hadn't been before. Lily reminded herself of his potential for being a psychopath, but the idea only heightened her desire for him. He didn't have to actually murder her... there were so many other ways he could kill her.

"You were close?" she asked, and cleared her throat to shuffle the thoughts from her mind. He punched a button to take them upstairs—to the second of three floors in this sprawling monster of a house.

"We were. My father was my best friend. He taught me everything I know."

Conversation fell aside as the doors opened and they entered a gallery of glass cases. Lily's eyes widened as she took in the collection.

"Oh, my God," she said with a breathy gasp, "how did you get all of this?"

"My father's legacy," Rowan said. "Please, have a look around."

Lily gasped, her eyes widening in awe. The items in the cases were breathtaking—bits of history thought to be lost forever. She recognized many of the pieces, from early Mesopotamian to late Renaissance, each piece carefully preserved. She wandered through the rows, lost in the sheer majesty of the collection until movement on the far end of the room caught her attention. She had all but forgotten her host, but he seemed to pay no mind. He appeared perfectly content to watch her.

There was something in his eyes that frightened her...something dark and powerful.

Possessive.

This was not good. She realized this interview absolutely was something else; something for which no amount of school could prepare her. Lily felt trapped, as if she'd been lured in with luxuries only to be stalked by something sinister. *Psychopath. Lunatic. Serial Killer.*

Shaking herself back to reality, she crossed the room to stand in front of him. She smiled as best she could while fighting to control the nervous shriek building in her throat.

"Thank you, Mr. Keir," she said briskly, "for a lovely time and the tea, but I'm afraid I can't work for you." She extended her hand to him, and he took it, his thumb grazing the sensitive flesh of her wrist.

"That is too bad," he said, regret tugging at the corners of his eyes. "But before you leave, might I ask why?"

Lily hesitated. Why did she want to leave? Was she afraid of him? Or was she afraid of herself if left in captivity with him for long periods of time? She didn't know anymore. What she did know was that he was very handsome and very, very tempting, and this situation was spiraling out of control. Fast.

"Let's just say it's a matter of trust," she said. "My mother always taught me to be wary of things that seem too good to be true."

"You do not trust me," he said, disappointment mixing with the regret on his face. He still held her hand, absently circling her skin with the pad of his thumb and sending little tingles of sensation coursing through her body. "I do apologize for that. Perhaps we should return to the sitting room to finish our discussion?"

"No," she said. "It isn't you I don't trust."

This revelation clearly puzzled him. His eyebrows knitted in confusion, and the left corner of his lip curled away from his teeth just enough to show the enamel behind it. "Who do you not trust, my dear?" There it was again…that unconscious affection which threatened her undoing. God, she was going to have to admit that she wanted him in a bad way.

"Myself," she said in a quiet voice, looking away. "I don't even know what this job is," she continued. "All I know is that you want a woman my age, you like a sense of humor, and you are obviously too wealthy for your own good because your private collection is more impressive than the Smithsonian!" Catching her own irritated reflection in the side of one of the display cases, Lily sighed and turned away from him. "I don't know what you could ever want with someone like me... I'm nothing."

"You could not be more wrong," he said, just behind her left ear. She jumped in surprise, once again very aware of his presence. "You, Lily Redway, are exactly what I have been looking for."

She snorted and took a few steps to put some distance between them. She glanced at her reflection again. She was what could only be described as average. Average height, average weight, with average-length brown hair, and a butt she was convinced was too big. She always liked her bright blue eyes, but compared to the sparkling depth of his, even those appeared dull. He could never want her the way she craved him.

"I have not been completely honest with you, I am afraid," Rowan said, again closing the distance between them. "I am looking for an assistant of sorts... A partner."

"You said that."

"But more than anything I am looking for a companion."

She turned then to glare at him. "A girlfriend?"

"For a bit," he admitted. "I need an assistant to manage my assets. Someone to talk to, to care about... and to one day care about me." His gaze tangled around hers, and she felt its pull despite the fury boiling in her gut. "I want a mate."

Lily's brain went into overdrive. Anger filled her chest, bleeding over into her eyes and coating her tongue with venom. She'd known it from the start. It was all a setup. She'd told herself over and over it couldn't be, that she was imagining the worst. Faced with the truth, she couldn't believe he thought this silly plan would work.

"You think it's all right to lure women in with your charm and wealth only to shoot them down because they aren't good enough for you? Is this your way of telling me to buzz off?"

"No," he said, extending his arms as if he were reaching for her. He stopped short, and dropped his hands back to his sides when she glared at him. "You are the only woman I have met in two months of searching whom I have even considered."

"That's supposed to be a compliment?"

"The highest."

She deflated. How could she argue with the sincerity in his tone?

"Let me take you to dinner," he said—almost pleaded. "Give me one more chance to explain all of this to you in a neutral setting. If you still wish to leave after you have heard my story, you can go and never look back." He turned his hand palm up to her. "Please, Lily."

She sighed.

Insanity.

That was the only way to describe what was going on. Complete and utter craziness. If she were smart, she would walk away, hormones be damned. Yet she couldn't muster the impetus to put one foot in front of the other.

"Last chance, but I expect real answers," she said, inwardly cringing at her own foolishness.

"Of course," he agreed, smiling when she took his hand.

Rowan led her through the labyrinthine hallways that made up his home—and this was his home, she realized as they passed through the massive, gourmet kitchen, pausing only long enough to remove the smoking jacket he wore and lay it across the back of a barstool before resuming his trek into the garage—all the while explaining various pieces of his collection. The small talk he offered only accentuated his nervousness. Lily wasn't sure she understood why he was trying so hard to impress her.

And she certainly wasn't going to admit that it was working.

Inside the cavernous garage he led her to a small, black two-seater, laid back the top, opened her door, and helped her inside. The manners were good, but she was still confused. He was going to explain the scenario to her—not that she particularly wanted to know what was going on.

When the car stopped, it was in front of an upscale bistro fourteen blocks from his home. A young man in a full tux opened her door and helped her out, then took Rowan's place behind the wheel. The car disappeared a moment later, leaving them standing on the sidewalk.

"I've never been here," Lily said. Now it was her turn to be nervous. "It looks expensive."

"No more than any other establishment I frequent. It is far less formal, however."

Lily's attitude flattened. "That's not exactly reassuring."

Rowan smiled. "Come on." He pulled open the door and led her inside.

The little restaurant was artfully decorated, the walls and floors covered in shabby-chic, mismatched furniture and decorations. Along the far wall sat three pastry cases, filled with the most delectable sights. A few people milled about, discussing their dessert choices as Rowan led her to a small table near the window.

A waitress materialized at Rowan's elbow, a bright smile turned on him. She appeared to not notice Lily's presence at all. If she had, she was certainly doing a good job of pretending otherwise. Rowan ordered a bottle of white wine and two glasses of water, then asked for the afternoon's special for both of them.

While his ordering for her was flattering, it was also slightly annoying. Such a move seemed pretentious considering they had only just met.

"It's easier to order the special than attempt to read a menu here," he said as if reading her mind. The sheepish, rakish grin he flashed was enough— Lily forgave him.

"Fair enough. So why are we here again?" she asked, letting her attention wander to their busy surroundings.

"I would like to apologize...first for the earlier deception," he said, bringing her thoughts back to the present and her gaze back to his. "But my luck is not what I would call the best." He relaxed down into the very old, very comfortable-looking wingback chair. This, she realized, was the real him, and cozy as it seemed, she wasn't about to fall into the trap again. "When I meet women in a non-professional setting, one of two things happens without fail."

"Let me guess," Lily stopped him by holding up her palm between them, "your wealth either intimidates or entices them." He looked up at her, surprised.

"Yes."

"Oh, please," she rolled her eyes, having lost interest in whatever game it was he was playing. She rose from her chair, angry. "Don't hand me that spoiled rich victim crap. Of course money attracts the wrong kinds! But that still doesn't give you the right to lure people in with the promise of a job."

It was his turn to sigh. "I know." Seeing the bereft look on his face, Lily deflated. She sighed and sank back into her chair. Heartbreak and loneliness flickered in his expression, which turned to surprise as she took his hand and patted it. His bare skin felt feverish.

"I get it," she said. "The world is tough, and we all do what we can to get by." She thumped his knuckles, making him cringe at the sudden sting. "But more money than God does not make up for such social ineptitude!"

He laughed out loud, a rich, hearty sound that surprised her and stirred her earlier feelings. It also temporarily stopped all movement in the building.

"You certainly do not mince words."

"I know." She paused then said, "It wasn't supposed to happen like this, was it? This plan of yours?"

Rowan shook his head. "No. It certainly was not." He turned her hand over in his and dragged his palm over the length of her fingers. His skin was smooth, yet the pads of his fingers were rough with calluses. Her whole arm tingled.

"You are an amazing woman, Lily." Her name rolled off his tongue like a caress. She swallowed, unable to hide the blush crawling up her neck.

"I've never heard that before."

"Why is there no man in your life?" His fingers still toyed with her hand and wrist. God, it was hard to think with him doing that. She didn't want to think at all despite the warning bells in her head. She had every intention of walking away, but now that the conversation had turned, escape would not be easy. Not that she wanted to escape anymore.

"Trust issues," she said, trying hard not to purr as his fingers tickled their way to her elbow. It was inappropriate, but it felt so good. "I always seem to walk into the wrong relationships." Rowan paused, and drew his hand back to hers.

"I am sorry, Lily."

"For what?"

"For betraying your trust." She started to speak when he held up his free hand to stop her, much as she had done to him moments earlier. "Let me finish, please." Her mouth snapped shut with an audible click of teeth. "From the moment you walked through my door I knew you were special. You were so much different than anyone else I have…" he hesitated, "interviewed." She bit back a pang of jealousy and her stomach flip-flopped at the thought that he'd given this speech more than once. She'd temporarily forgotten that this was an interview for the position of wife. "You carried yourself so gracefully. You have the intelligence to back up the mischief I see dancing in your eyes... I should have told you from the start what my intentions were. I should have been clear that I want more than an employee."

"Am I allowed to speak now?"

Rowan smiled. "Of course. What else would you like to know? What would I need to do to make you stay?"

"First, you know this doesn't have a snowball's chance in hell of working, right?"

"I had the feeling," he said with a dry, brittle smirk.

"Now, I'm going to tell you why."

"Please do."

"Three reasons. First, you, at this moment, are too good to be true."

"That, I can assure you, is not the case. I have my flaws."

"Second," she continued with a pointed glare, "you are a very dangerous man."

"How so?"

"That is the third reason. If I intend to work for you, I can't have a physical relationship with you. And you doing that," she wiggled the fingers still clasped in his, "makes it very difficult to think of anything but."

"So this job... You do understand that there is no clearly defined employment opportunity, right?"

"Oh, yes, there is," Lily retorted. "You don't even see the opportunity, do you?" Rowan shook his head slowly, as if he wasn't following. His smile faltered. "You have the most amazing collection of artifacts I've ever seen. You need someone to catalog them and put them on display for you. The world needs to see it. I can do it for you, but I can't be your beck-and-call-girl and a professional personal assistant all at once."

"Fair enough," he mused, that thin smile still playing at the corners of his mouth, revealing dimples. He was trying to kill her...she knew it. Lily closed her eyes and cleared her throat. When she looked up again, the waitress was filling Rowan's glass from the frosty wine bottle. She conveniently left Lily's glass empty. Rowan scowled and pulled the bottle from her hand. "Now answer a question for me," he continued, fixing Lily with a sharp stare.

"Okay," she croaked.

A smile spread across his face, slow and devious. "How am I dangerous?"

"Power, wealth, and charm," she said through clenched teeth and took the glass he offered. "No man should have all three."

"Which says nothing at all about my ravishing good looks."

"Exactly," Lily replied, staring at him with smoldering eyes. Rowan blinked in obvious surprise.

"You do know I was kidding?"

"Then you've obviously never looked in a mirror."

Something shifted between them. Lily felt the power surge around her, knowing his desire just as strong and clear as she felt her own. She swallowed the lump in her throat, tensing as he leaned toward her.

The waitress, to Lily's great chagrin, interrupted the moment by placing their food on the table. Rowan's meal consisted of the most artistic sandwich, salad and soup combination she'd ever seen, while hers appeared slapped together and tossed around on the plate. What may once have been a beautiful meal worried her. If Lily lifted the lettuce, she worried she might find an unwanted gift, and she had the sneaking suspicion it had everything to do with her choice of company. It was obvious the girl carried a torch for him even if he ignored her.

How he could watch her with such adoration was beyond Lily's comprehension. Shifting uncomfortably, she scooped the sandwich up as best she could, prepared to eat though it appeared her food had already been chewed a few times, when Rowan's hand landed on her wrist.

"Wait a minute," he said, examining her food with a look of disgust. "Give me your plate." She laid the sandwich down and handed it over. Calm and silent, Rowan stood and took her food back to the small window that acted as a pass. After a heated discussion with whoever was on the other side of the wall, he returned, a new plate in his hands that looked worlds different from what the waitress had given her.

"You didn't have to do that," she said as he laid it in front of her. "I was going to eat it."

"I would not let you."

"Why not? It's just food."

"It was tainted." His gaze darkened, and just like that his good humor was gone. Rowan planted himself in his chair and picked up his own sandwich.

Tainted? she wondered. *How would he know that?*

"Do not ask, Lily. Just eat so we can leave."

They ate quickly and in eerie silence. His outburst seemed to have stilled the restaurant yet again. Before she'd even finished chewing, Rowan had her by the arm, pulling her out of the door without even bothering to stop and pay a bill. She had to jog to keep up with his long strides, and when he deposited her into his car, she was breathing so heavily that her vision was blurred.

He was already stopping the car before she was able to catch her breath again. "Where are we?" she gasped, which seemed to pause him in his single-minded mission. His face fell blank, and his whole demeanor shifted.

"Away from that horrid woman," he replied. His nostrils flared with one last hint of residual anger, but when he looked over at her, only the warm humor from earlier remained. My home is just around the corner. I thought it best if I deliver you back to civilization and your means of escape before I decide to keep you forever."

An anticipatory thrill ran up and down her spine. Absurd, but she liked the idea of being his kept woman. Sort of—with some freedom, of course, but to be his could be fun.

"Perhaps you would like to come back inside for a drink?" he asked as he maneuvered the car into the garage and killed the engine. Common sense told her she should say goodnight, leave, and continue her job search in the morning. Lily wasn't cut out for his lifestyle. However, her intentions were far different than her common sense dictated.

"I would love that."

"Fabulous." Rowan exited the car, and before she could remove her seatbelt was pulling open her door and offering his hand. Lily took it, exciting in the jolt of energy that passed between them. Logically, she knew this was a bad idea and knew what could happen. What would happen.

But she didn't care. She allowed him to pull her from the seat and lead her inside, stopping only long enough to proffer another bottle of wine from a hidden refrigerator and two glasses from the overhead rack. He took her hand again, and tugged her out of the darkened kitchen.

Lily scarcely noticed her surroundings as he led her up a staircase and into a different part of the building—his home. The whole building, half a city block. That realization was overwhelming.

The stairwell opened into a high-ceilinged room, lavishly decorated with the same cozy antiques as the rest of the house, but this new area felt warm and lived-in. Behind her, Lily heard the pop of the cork, and the soft *glug-glug* of wine filling the glasses. Rowan appeared at her side a moment later and pressed one of the glasses into her hand. He raised his toward her.

"A toast to interesting conversation and a new beginning." The warm smile on his face melted her reservations, and she touched her glass to his.

"To new beginnings," she echoed and drank. When she lowered her glass, Rowan was watching her intently. Arousal burned in his pale eyes, and the strength of his determination raised the hairs along her arms. Lily swallowed as he leaned toward her one more time.

CHAPTER THREE

"I am going to kiss you," Rowan whispered, and she nodded just as his lips met hers. It started as a light flutter of pressure in a chaste brush of his mouth. His warm fingers brushed her throat and she gasped. Bracing his palm against the nape of her neck, Rowan crushed his mouth to hers, sweeping his tongue across her lips before plunging inside and tangling with her own.

When he pulled away, they were both breathless. The bowl of her glass dangled limply from the tips of her fingers, the last drops of wine threatening to drip out onto the carpet as she braced herself on his forearms, strong and muscular through the thick sleeves of his coat.

"I am sorry," he whispered, leaning his forehead against hers. His voice was little more than a husky growl. "That was highly inappropriate."

"Yes," she gasped. "Do it again."

Rowan laughed as he cradled her head in his free hand and pulled back to look at her. "You said this would ruin our working relationship."

"No, I said I wouldn't work for you."

"Are you saying you have forgiven me for my earlier untruths?"

"Not yet," she said sternly, and pressed a gentle hand to his chest. She drained the final bit of liquid from her glass. "So you have a lot of groveling to do."

"Gladly," he said with a groan and pulled her flush against him. Their lips met once more with a jolt of passionate energy and she vaguely heard the tinkling of glass on the floor as his dropped glass shattered. Rowan crushed her against his chest. Through the thin fabric of her blouse she could feel the heat of his body, pulsing with the frantic beat of his heart. Her own battered out an uneven, excited rhythm as she wound her arms around him, tugging the tie and pulling it loose from the collar of his deep green satin shirt. Her fingers bunched in the fabric, pulling him closer. His hands found her hips, fingers digging into the sensitive flesh there as he tugged her first to a nearby settee, then to straddle his lap. Beneath their combined weight, the legs of the antique sofa groaned, snatching them both out of the moment.

Rowan chuckled against her neck. "I suppose this is not the best place for such activity." Lily avoided his eyes, a blush blooming on her cheeks. Her gaze raked over his kiss-swollen lips. He looked even more enticing. She hadn't thought that possible.

Then the reality set in. She was straddling the lap of a man she did not know, all too eager to have sex with him. This was not her. But the things he did to her...just the touch of his fingertips on her cheek ignited a frenzy she'd never felt before.

Fighting panic, Lily shimmied backwards, finding her footing before hauling herself out of his arms and across the room.

"I'm sorry," she said quietly. "I got a little carried away." Still, she refused to look at Rowan, despite his attempts to catch her eye.

"Lily, look at me," he coaxed, adjusting his shirt as he rose from the couch. Reluctantly, she cast her gaze up at him. "You have nothing to apologize for." He took a step toward her and she took one backward. "I fear it is I who should apologize to you."

The comment startled her. "For what?"

"I should have let you leave when you first asked to do so." His face flushed and his stare burned. "But you are so beautiful...so intelligent...so...right." He took a deep breath, inhaling her essence. "The thought of you walking out my door and never returning is heartbreaking."

Lily chewed her bottom lip. No man had ever said such things to her, and certainly not with such conviction. Rowan watched her, his eyes fixed on her teeth as they worried the sensitive skin between them.

"You don't know what you're saying," Lily said quietly, and re-twisted the chignon on the back of her head. She clutched the chopsticks between her teeth as she did so. Rowan sucked in a breath. "What?"

"You tempt me," he admitted. "I do not deserve you."

"Why?" She pulled the sticks from her mouth and went back to chewing her lip as she secured her hair in place.

"My mother raised me a gentleman, Lily. I have been foolish and taken advantage of you." He watched her through narrowed eyelids. "And unless you stop doing that, I may not be able to stop from doing so again."

Lily let go of her lip with an audible pop. His intense gaze burned. She felt like she was under a microscope. "I'm sorry," she said. She licked her lips and swallowed hard. Rowan groaned.

"You really are making this so difficult," he said, and drew in a hard breath through his nose. "If you intend to leave," he continued, closing the distance between them in two strides, "you should do it now because I am going to kiss you again, and once I do I will not be able to stop."

Lily floundered for words, and found none. She wanted him; there was no way to deny it. He moved toward her, backing her against the wall where he pressed his body against hers.

"Last chance," he breathed. The look in his eyes was feral. It frightened her. There was a hunger unlike any other she'd ever seen. Her mouth opened, but no response came out. Rowan smiled, cradled her face in one hand, and bent to kiss her. The touch was gentle and filled with restraint. He was being careful with her.

Lily discovered in that moment that she was tired of careful. No man had ever shown such interest in her, so she no longer cared about propriety. She was jobless, on the verge of being homeless, and without a single redeeming prospect. She needed the release, and right now all she cared about was having him in the most intimate way possible. As her inhibitions melted, so did his restraint. Tightening his hands on her, Rowan forced her mouth open, possessing her with a hungry growl. She let him lead, let him tug her away from the wall and hard against the length of his body. His arms wound around her as he tasted her. Rowan lifted her like she were no heavier than a ragdoll, and again she followed his lead, twisting her legs around his waist. Without releasing her mouth, he turned and carried her into another room. Then she felt the softness of a down mattress beneath her and the weight of his body on top of her. Warm, wet lips trailed down her throat and over her collar bone. She gasped as the fabric of her blouse parted enough for his fingers to tickle across her ribcage.

"There is more you need to know," he growled against her, his mouth still occupied by her skin.

"Later…" she gasped. She wanted to speak more but couldn't find the courage to say his name. Even if she had been able to find her voice, he'd have taken it away again as his teeth grazed the soft flesh above her left breast. He growled something against her skin, and Lily's hands moved from his shoulders to stroke across the top of his head—something she'd wanted to do since the first time she laid eyes on him. His hair was longer than she thought, thick and soft against her palms.

The sound of ripping fabric echoed in the quiet room, and his fingers danced across her now bare nipples. Lily closed her eyes against the sensations, gasping when the sharp points of his teeth grazed the places his fingers had been.

Rowan rocked back and knelt over her, his gaze smoky. She felt very self-conscious splayed out before him. A growl started low in his chest, rumbling out through him as he loosed the buttons of his shirt. She took a deep breath and watched, rapt, as his chest came slowly into view. On his knees above her, he was a god in flesh, his arms, chest, and throat snaked with tribal tattoos interspersed with scars. This man looked as if he'd seen battle.

"Wow…" she breathed, and sat up, reaching for him. Fingers hesitating, she swallowed and made contact with his skin. Beneath the soft exterior and the raised scars, his body was hard and flawless, his skin tanned and perfect, velvet beneath her fingertips. She leaned forward, brushing her lips along the deepest of the scars. The smell of him—woodsy musk mixed with hints of expensive cologne—filled her senses. He clutched at the back of her head, pulling the sticks from her hair and loosening it from its neat knot to let it thread through his fingers. Lily sighed, and with a tentative kiss, drew her tongue over his scarred skin. Rowan moaned. The sound empowered her, giving her the courage to slide her fingers along his sides, tracing the tattoos as she moved over his chest and up his shoulders, coming to points just behind his ears. As she explored his body, his own hands moved over her, curling around to weigh her heavy breasts and tug at her nipples.

Pushing against her hands, Rowan leaned in and kissed her again. He traced his tongue along her lips before fully possessing her mouth again, driving her back against the mattress.

His skin burned against hers. Every place he touched ignited a fire that pooled low in her belly, every place his lips grazed shot tingles to her center. All coherent thought stopped as his lips descended on her inner thigh. Hot fingers clasped her hips tightly, stilling her while his lips moved slowly toward her center. Lily gasped, fingers bunching in the sheets beneath her. His breath tickled over her, making her squirm in his grasp. A warm tongue traced the line of her opening, deftly slipping between her lips to her core. She squealed, and he groaned against her as if he were a starving man at a feast.

Rowan ground his lips against her, drove his tongue into her, slipped his teeth over the sensitive nub of flesh he found buried there. Lily writhed and moaned as he pushed her closer and closer to the edge, only to pull her back and start over. Several times he drove her to the breaking point, only to tease her back down. Her gaze locked with his as he slipped one finger inside her, drawing it back before pushing in again. Her hips rose and fell in time with his movements, the delicious friction of his tongue pressing against her turning her bones to mush. Drawing her into his mouth, he suckled hard and curled his fingers up, stroking a hidden, sensitive spot inside her. Lily gasped, the breath rushing from her lungs as her body coiled around itself with each deft stroke of his fingers deep inside her. And when she came, it was as if she'd flown apart at the seams.

"You taste wonderful," he breathed as he crawled up her body. "You must feel even better." He kissed her again as he flexed his hips, pressing his clothed length against her. Lily moaned into his lips, the taste of herself on his tongue and the feeling of his weight crushing her down pushing her back to that edge and giving her the strength to push him over. He gave in, stretching languidly beneath her gaze as she drew her fingertips down his body, chasing them with her lips.

With shaking hands, she pulled free the button of his pants and snaked her hand inside. To her surprise he wore nothing underneath, and her fingers met with his hard, feverish length. Breath hissed between his teeth when her hand smoothed over the soft head of his cock. She wrapped her fingers around his width and stroked. She swore his eyes crossed as she toyed with him, his hips pumping up against her fist in time with her movements. With her free hand, Lily eased the zipper of his pants down, freeing both her hand and his erection to the cool air.

Lily released him to hook her fingers in the waistband of his pants and draw them down his hips and off. Rowan raised his head and watched her as she tickled her fingers over his bare thighs. She slicked her palms over his hips, her long, slender fingers grasping at him once again. Lily bent, flicking her tongue against the sensitive head of his cock, tasting the salty fluid gathered there. He growled, tangling his hands in her hair, and tugged her up his body to capture his mouth. The rough growth of his facial hair scratched at her cheeks—had it been that long before?—as he crushed her against him and rolled her onto her back.

Breath left her in a rush when the full weight of his body bore down on her. His hands and mouth seemed everywhere at once. Her fingernails dug into his shoulders, urging him on, begging him for more. Something resembling a snarl tore from his lips as he hooked one knee under her thigh and drove deep into her. Lily screamed, the feel of him so suddenly filling and stretching her a shock. Her inner muscles clamped down on him greedily, pulling him deeper.

Rowan pulled back and pushed forward again, the muscles in his arms bunching on either side of her as he lifted himself to look down at her. Every cell in her body shivered with delight at each thrust of his cock deep into her womb, every muffled groan and growl from his throat. Her body curled and tightened around him in a dance of the most exquisite torture, dragging him deeper, begging him for more. She shook with need, her legs winding around his waist as her fingernails clawed into his arms. Lights flashed behind her eyes and the edges of her consciousness darkened as the first spasm hit, then closing in with each pleasure-filled shudder of her body. Rowan growled, hands clutching hard at her body and he jerked once, then crushed himself against her in release, pouring into her with a triumphant howl. The last thing Lily knew was the feeling of his fingers relaxing their bruising hold and a rush of cold wind before she slipped into darkness.

CHAPTER FOUR

Consciousness came back to her slowly. Images from the night before and Rowan's determined lovemaking filtered through the haze in her head. She'd met consciousness twice before, only to be dragged back into oblivion by five of the most powerful orgasms she'd ever experienced.

Lily tested her limbs, unsure their dead weight could move, and found a pleasant ache crawling over her body. The satisfied pain was dotted with a more acute hurt, centered on each of her hips. Bruises, no doubt, from Rowan's eager climax.

Pushing back the sheet, Lily gasped. A mix of shock and horror washed over her as she looked down at her battered, bruised body and the raw gashes caked with dried blood on her hips. Moving away from her place in the bed were deep gashes, claw marks shredding the down mattress. Strips were gouged out of the hardwood floors, and a light dusting of feathers had settled over everything in the room. Bits of white fluff clung to the ends of her hair and stuck to the bloody patches on her skin. Up and down her arms and torso, small, purple blossoms grew.

"What...the hell?" she breathed, slipping out of the bed on the opposite side of the ruined spot. Her clothes lay in pieces, scattered about the room. The shirt Rowan wore lay draped over the chair, and she slipped it over her shoulders, trying to ignore the spicy, woodsy scent that still clung to it. Despite the carnage, her sex tingled at the thought of him.

The shirt swallowed her. He was every bit a big man, and the way the fabric hung from her body made her feel small and feminine. All she could think was how nice it would be to crawl back into the bed and into his arms, but her sensible side quickly latched onto the mess of her surroundings and reminded her that she needed answers.

On the far wall was a large window, covered by heavy drapes. There was no clock. No television. No electronics of any sort; nothing to tell her the time. Her purse was lost somewhere in the house, along with her host. Carefully picking her way across the room to avoid the damage, she pulled back the drapes to overlook the back side of the building and the park across the street.

On the horizon, the soft glow of morning crawled over the city, and one by one the streetlights below winked out. How long had she been sleeping? Her appointment was at 4:00 and then he had taken her to dinner...*the previous evening,* she thought.

On the inside of the stone wall surrounding the city block was a private garden, hidden from the rest of the world. A figure lay beneath a small dogwood tree, unmoving. She couldn't be certain from this height, but it looked like Rowan. Whoever he was, he looked to be in pain. If it was Rowan, Lily wanted to help him...but still she hesitated. If it had been Rowan that caused the damage...

No, aching hips or not, he couldn't have shredded the bed and the floor that way. Only an animal could have caused that damage, and she was far too practical to even consider the possibility of Rowan being a...

Werewolf.

Lily stumbled over the word even in her thoughts. Talk about a ridiculous idea—things like that didn't exist. Besides, the full moon wasn't for another week at least. That damage must have already been there and she was too distracted to notice. Still, that didn't explain how she ended up covered in mattress feathers. Besides, he was wealthy. He would have had that damage repaired before he let anyone in.

Maybe he had a dog she didn't know about. He did say he had a pet. It could have come in and done the damage while she was sleeping. But even that wouldn't work. Lily was a light sleeper, and any sound like that would have awoken her, particularly in a strange place. Still, the memory of the noises he made at the point of climax haunted the edges of her thoughts. He'd sounded so much like an animal the night before...

Lily shoved the thoughts from her mind and went to find the elevator, at the same time hoping and fearing she was alone with him. The house was a maze of hallways and rooms, each connected to all of the others. Lily stumbled upon the gallery by accident, and quickly found that the elevator that took her back downstairs did not exit into the rear courtyard. In a frustrated last attempt, she wound her way back through to the sitting room with the Monet, and went out the door Rowan had first entered.

This door took her down a long hallway full of closed doors that finally, mercifully, exited into the courtyard. The sun had not risen, but the sky was streaked with the gentle pastels of morning, casting a pale glow over the whole of the garden. The air was cool and fresh, and the trees dripped tiny jewels of water—early Spring rain.

The figure under the tree was indeed Rowan, lying on his side, naked, in a fetal position. She padded across the dewy grass, moving toward him. He appeared to be sleeping, but as she neared she noticed his chest hitching with occasional uneven breaths. Was he crying?

"Rowan?" she asked softly. "What is it?"

"Go back inside!" he snarled, and seemed to curl in tighter on himself.

"What's wrong?" she pushed, ignoring his demand and inched closer. "What can I do to help?"

A low, keening wail escaped his throat. "You cannot," he rasped. His voice grew hard and cold. "Go inside and go back to bed." As the sky lightened she noticed the tattoos running down his back and legs to match those on his chest, and how most of them were obscured by cakes of dried mud.

"I can't just leave you like this," she said, and crouched over him. Lily took him by the shoulder, recoiling from the heat of his skin. "You're burning up! We need to get you to a hospital!"

"No," he gasped, pulling away from her.

"Rowan, this isn't right." She closed her hands on his shoulder and pulled him back to face her. Her breath caught in her throat as his body came into view. What she thought was dirt, she realized, was dried blood on his skin. A fine misting of dark hair covered his chest and arms — she'd been close enough that she was certain it had not been there before. Lily's hand flew to her mouth to stifle a scream as she took in his fingers; distended, gnarled and bloody. Sharp, heavy claws peeled back the skin at his fingertips. As she watched, they shrank back into his hands, the skin sealing itself over and stopping the pour of blood. Within moments, those hands were the same that had held her so gently the night before. "Rowan," she gasped, slipping backwards on the wet grass.

"I told you to go back inside," he breathed. His body convulsed in pain and a sharp cry tore from his throat. The sound sent Lily running, escaping back into the house and away from the monster that lay outside. She started for the front door, then remembered her things upstairs. There was likely no way he could get up and catch her before she got to her purse and out the door again.

Rowan heaved his bulk into a seated position. His head ached and his body felt tight. He couldn't remember the last time he'd felt so good and so awful at the same time. It had been decades, at least. Maybe longer. He'd bedded women time and again, but he could never remember a climax bringing on the change, and he could never remember quite so violent a change. And now the woman responsible for his mindlessness was lost somewhere in the maze of his home, looking for any means of escape.

A shock of pain coursed up his spine into the base of his head and he cradled his face with his hands, drawing a sharp breath to offset the sting. Adrenaline still rushed; the after-effects of his shift. He'd hoped to be clear of the change and back inside to clean up before she woke, but this time the comedown had taken longer than ever...too long, as it turned out. He was just thankful she didn't wake before. He'd have had no way at all of explaining away the wolf in his private courtyard. Or where he was while the wolf was there. Or where the wolf went when he reappeared.

Rowan rose from the ground, brushing away the caked, dried dirt and blood from his bare body, and stalked inside. His muscles still ached but the excitement faded. He'd been so close with her — if only he'd been able to keep the monster at bay, he might have had a real chance with Lily. His intentions truly were twofold — he needed someone to keep after him and keep up with him, but also to watch out for him during the times when he wasn't human. However, with her…

With her, he envisioned a life.

The gentle scent of strawberries still hung in the air of the house, more and more concentrated as he exited the stairwell into the sitting room just outside his bedroom. She'd only been here moments before. The air was still warm and swirling, and bits of down danced across the floor where she'd no doubt picked them off of herself. He smiled, even as the thought stung his heart. She was no doubt already gone, and there would be little chance of catching her. Even less chance of making her stay, he knew.

Rowan sighed and entered his closet, grabbing a towel and a fresh set of clothes then trudged off toward the bathroom. He'd have to clean the mess, but until her scent was a little less conspicuous, it would have to wait.

Lily's hands shook as she gripped the steering wheel of her car. She still hadn't moved from the parking garage down the street, hadn't even moved to put the key in the ignition and turn it on. Despite the shock she'd just received, her mind was blank. She couldn't even think, much less perform a complicated task like drive while a single thought bounced around her brain: Things like this were not supposed to happen. People were not supposed to be able to turn into animals. That was best left for scary stories and horror movies... She just couldn't reconcile the fact that Rowan's hands had shifted all on their own.

With a small whimper, Lily shoved the key into the ignition and turned it. She stared forward at the empty, concrete wall of the parking deck, trying to convince herself she needed to just leave the city. Lily told herself to go home, take a long, hot bath, and relax. It was Friday, and she didn't have anywhere to be. She needed to take a day or two and reset. Forget about Rowan Keir and his...illness.

And about the night of incredible sex.

She moaned and covered her face with her hands. Lily hated being so confused...so torn. On one hand, she wanted to run away and never look back. But she also wanted more of his attention. And she couldn't forget the pained look on his face just before she turned tail and ran. She wanted to help him.

While she battled with her emotions, her car made the decision for her. Its spluttering engine gave a sharp, loud cough, wheezed, and died.

"No!" she cried, trying the key again. It revved, then clicked and made no more noise. "No, no, no!" No matter how she turned the key, the engine refused to turn over. She whimpered, crossing her arms on the steering wheel and laying her head against their crux. "Why is this happening?"

She couldn't very well go into one of the businesses dressed the way she was—in only a too-large shirt that belonged to a man she hardly knew. She could call a tow truck, but her cell was dead and she had no outside communication with the world.

That left only one option.

Heaving a deep sigh, Lily threw open her car door, snatched up her purse, and trudged back toward her fate.

Rowan lay sprawled in an armchair, one wrist thrown across his eyes to shield the lamplight in the corner. His head pounded in time with his heartbeat, and over and over the image of Lily's pretty face screwed up in terror floated through his mind's eye.

It appeared he would have to post another ad… or maybe he was doomed to be alone. After all, the best thing to ever come into his life was now gone. Just as well…he wasn't quite sure how he was going to explain that while the older pieces of the collection were his father's, he'd been the one to purchase the majority of them.

When they were first crafted.

If she'd been horrified by the sight of him in half-shift, she would no doubt be shocked beyond comprehension to discover that his birth took place just as the great Renaissance artists were discovering themselves. And if Loki were to find him again…he could not reasonably subject her to that sort of horror.

After over six centuries of near solitude, Rowan thought himself an imbecile to believe she could be the one to give him the peace he so desperately sought.

A knock on the lobby door interrupted his thoughts. It was odd that someone would wander into the building like that…likely someone looking for directions. People never visited this building, despite the front door always being unlocked. Rowan heaved himself from the chair and crossed the room to shoo the intruder.

"Lily?" He was shocked to find her standing there, still in his shirt. "I thought I would never see you again."

"I need to borrow a phone," she said, her voice icy. Rowan stepped back out of her way and allowed her inside, his heart sinking at her chilly tone.

"Are you having trouble?"

"My car broke down."

"Then perhaps I—" he started, but she held up a hand to stop him.

"No. Just let me use your telephone and I will be out of your hair in five minutes."

Rowan sighed, and turned for the door. No use in arguing. "Come on," he muttered, and led her through the back hallway, up the stairs and into the back portion of the house. He pointed to the telephone sitting on the counter of his kitchen, and she breezed past him without a word, reaching for the receiver. The scent of strawberries and sex wafted through the air at her passing, stirring up dominant, possessive feelings.

His hands clenched at his sides as she spoke into the phone. The voice on the other end was male, and the thought of her speaking to another man put his temper on the rise. He wanted to throw the phone across the room, to hold her down and make her understand how much he needed her.

She made a low noise and slammed the phone down. Rowan stood by, hoping she would ask his help, just to have an invitation to talk to her. She refused to turn around, opting instead to tug at her hair in frustration.

61

"What is it?" he asked, holding onto the tentative hope that he could draw her into conversation.

"It'll be an hour before they can tow my car back to my house."

"To your house?"

"Yeah. I'm currently without a job," she sighed. "I don't have the money to get it fixed."

"Let me call my mechanic," Rowan offered, and received a glare for his trouble.

"No."

"Please, Lily... It is the least I can do."

"I don't want your charity."

"This is not charity. You came here under the impression that you would have a job—which you can still have if you want it. Let me have your vehicle repaired. That is the least I can do for taking a day out of your search."

"Listen, Rowan, I appreciate the offer, but..." She paused, staring up at him with a confused look on her face and a delicate shudder shaking her shoulders.

"At least give me a chance to explain. And to get you a fresh set of clothes."

There it was again...that pain, etched so clearly into his eyes that it pulled at her heart. She wanted to be repulsed, to curl into herself and hide until the tow truck came to take her away from this place. But looking at the hurt on his face, she couldn't help but feel the need to comfort him. Lily crossed her arms over her chest and fought the urge to go to him.

"You have until the truck gets here," she said, knowing the chilly tone in her voice was undeserved. Was it really? she asked herself. After all, he'd not told her a thing about himself before taking her to bed.

But he had tried to tell her. It was her fault for stopping him. She'd told him to tell her later because she'd been so absorbed in the budding physical relationship that she didn't care about words. Never had she been so eager to get in someone's pants before. Shame burned her cheeks, and she tried to force away the thoughts of her depravity.

"Come with me," he said, his tone gentle and coaxing. "Let me get you fresh clothes."

Against her better judgment, Lily followed Rowan back through the house and into his bedroom. The feathers had been cleaned and the bed made—she had to wonder if he kept stacks of mattresses hidden somewhere just for the occasions when he tore them to shreds. The marks on the floor were hidden by an area rug, and despite her attempts to ignore it, her eyes still traveled back to the center of the bed…where she'd spent the night in his arms and woken up alone. Beneath the shirt, the scratches on her hips ached.

"I am afraid I do not have women's clothing lying about," he said, breaking her concentration, "but I hope these will not be too big on you." He handed her a pair of jogging pants and a T-shirt. "I do apologize for your clothing. I will have it replaced."

"Don't worry about it," she heard herself say, and wondered where her voice was coming from.

"The wash room is through that door." He pointed to a paneled door the same color as the walls. "I will fix you some breakfast while you clean up." Before she could argue, he disappeared, pulling the door closed behind him.

A sharp chill ran up Lily's spine.

This was not how she meant for things to happen. From the time she'd left the house, Lily intended to walk out of his life and never return, yet here she was again in his bedroom. With him going downstairs to cook her breakfast.

Lily didn't feel much like eating.

As her thoughts battled her hormones, she closed the bathroom door and turned on the water as hot as it could go. Which, as it turned out, was pretty damn hot. Turning it back to avoid scalding herself, she grabbed a cloth from the basket on the counter and used the hand-soap to clean the wounds on her hips. Each one, she found, was a small, round prick about the size of a pen-tip. They had already clotted over and begun to scab, but the warm water stung anyway. More bruises blossomed up and down her body, finger-sized marks that showed her just how possessive his lovemaking had been. She remembered the feel of his hands on her, the raw energy coursing between them and the need to feel him control her.

Frustrated with herself for falling back into the memories, Lily threw the rag into the sink, dried her body off, and pulled on the clothes he'd given her. When she opened the bathroom door, the smell of bacon slammed into her empty belly.

Rowan had to force himself not to stare at her when she came into the kitchen wearing his clothes. She'd had to roll the pants at her waist to keep them from dragging the floor, but the T-shirt fell over the curves of her breasts so deliciously that he had to shake himself back to reality. She still carried herself as if poised to run at any moment. Even as she perched on one of the bar stools at the island, she sat lightly with every muscle in her arms and legs singing with tension. He didn't blame her. He had a lot to tell her, and he was certain that telling her he'd upended her plans with the tow truck would make her angry.

"I need to apologize to you again," Rowan said as he flipped eggs into a hot pan. They sizzled and popped, and from across the room he heard her stomach rumble. "I never intended for things to happen like this. I never meant to frighten or harm you." Lily remained silent. As he glanced at her out of the corner of his eye, he realized she was again curling in on herself. She feared him. "I had hoped to have more time to explain my...situation," he continued. "You should not have seen what you did this morning." He turned around with a plate of food and crossed the room. She leaned away from him as he placed it in front of her. "There is no excuse for my behavior."

She looked at the plate then glanced up at him. Her stomach argued against her resolve, and ultimately won as she picked up a strip of bacon and bit the end off of it. He moved around the island to sit in front of her. She nibbled the bacon, looking everywhere but at him. Her mind was racing, he knew. She'd done the same thing while making up her mind the previous night.

"Lily?" he asked. "Look at me." She blinked, froze, and raised her eyes to meet his. "I am sorry."

"I know," she whispered, and looked away again. She eyed the plate, but did not move to pick anything else up from it. Everything about her screamed that she had something to say, but he had no idea how to make her say it. Finally, after six agonizing minutes, she cleared her throat and whispered, "What are you?"

Rowan cringed. Part of him knew it was coming, but he still wasn't prepared for the reality.

"A shape-shifter," he said, his voice cracking. "My parents were both bred from wolves."

A disbelieving bark of laughter erupted from her throat. "You're joking, right?"

"I wish I was. What you saw this morning was the most surprising change I have ever experienced."

She dared a look up at him, and as their eyes met, something in her face softened. He was willing to give anything to know what thoughts danced around in her head. She stared at him for a long, silent moment. Her blue eyes twinkled in the bright kitchen lights, and she reached for another strip of bacon.

"What exactly do you mean 'surprising'?" she asked.

"Being with you as we were last night forced a change in me." He swallowed and kept his gaze level with hers. "In all my years in this life, I have never experienced a shift in quite that way."

She blinked at him, her mouth falling open slightly. "What does that mean?"

"I wish I knew," he replied. "I would give anything to know." Rising from his seat, Rowan stalked around the island to stand beside her. Lily stared up at him, her eyes wide and a little terrified. He took her hand and placed it, fingers splayed, in the center of his chest. "I just know what you do to me."

Lily cleared her throat. "What...what is that?" she asked timidly. Rowan smiled.

"You make me want to protect and possess you all at once. To dominate and be dominated. You," he placed his fingers under her chin and lifted it as he stepped between her outstretched legs, "make me want you." He bent and brushed his mouth across hers, just the lightest of fluttering kisses. Finding no opposition, he cradled her head with one hand, slanting his mouth over hers to claim her again. Despite the flavor of cooked meat on her tongue, she still tasted as sweet and wild as she had the night before, and every bit as delectable.

She shoved him away and stumbled back from the island. "I can't do this," she cried, skittering toward the door. "It's all too much for me right now." She turned and pulled the door open. "Thank you for breakfast...and for last night. But I have to go meet the tow truck."

"Lily, wait," he called. For a moment he didn't think she would stop, but she paused just outside the door. "I have something else to tell you."

"What?" Her voice cracked.

"The tow truck is not coming." She wheeled around and stared at him, flames rising in her eyes as her face bloomed bright red. "I cancelled the tow to your house and had my personal mechanic pick it up. It will be ready for you this afternoon."

"You did it anyway," she hissed. "I should call the police for kidnapping and theft."

"Please," he gasped, fighting the urge to go to her and take her in his arms, "let me do this for you. And while your car is being repaired, let me take you to replace your clothes." He held his arms up in surrender. "I swear I will keep my hands to myself."

Lily closed her eyes and took a deep breath. He was so genuine about everything he said, but he was also a monster. He was a thing from camp-fire stories and children's nightmares. Yet he stood before her, his large, pale blue eyes begging her to stay. Her fight-or-flight instincts told her to fly—to run far away and never return…but he had her car. And he wanted to buy her clothes… It was such a weird situation.

"I don't know," she sighed. Her feet seemed glued to the floor, unable to move in either direction.

"Come on, Lily. Let me repay you for everything you have done for me. The least I can do is replace the clothing I destroyed." At the mention of it, her body tingled with excitement. How could she still want him so much after everything she'd seen? Her body very obviously didn't understand that her mind was not happy. She was trapped with him for a few hours anyway...why not listen to her body and make the best of it?

"All right."

Rowan rushed across the room as if he would hug her, only stopping short several feet. A lopsided grin curled his mouth and he held his hands up again. "I promised I'd keep my hands to myself." The comment made her smile, and deep in the pit of her stomach a small bloom of warmth spread its tendrils.

CHAPTER FIVE

Shopping with Rowan was more fun than Lily imagined it could be. Every article of clothing he picked up fit her as if it were made only for her. No matter how she argued, he continued to throw clothes at her, picking out his favorites while creating a large discard pile near her feet. She agreed to one set of clothes, but he insisted on more, simply because he thought they flattered her. In the end, the bill from the posh little boutique totaled more than her last two paychecks combined. Lily tried to argue, to demand that the clothing go back and they find the nearest department store, but he ignored her in favor of handing over one of the many credit cards tucked inside his wallet.

To further her financial discomfort, he insisted on buying shoes in a neighboring store to match the clothes, and lunch on the river at an upscale restaurant she never would have imagined entering while alone. With the money he spent, Lily had a hard time being angry with him over the issue of his nature. Instead she chose to be angry with him for not appreciating the value of money, and for throwing it around to impress her.

"So is this all a ploy to distract me?" she asked, ducking under his arm to enter the restaurant.

He grinned. "Something like that." Within moments they were led to a table in a bright, windowed corner. "Before you argue with me further," he said, "I do not intend to buy forgiveness. I do not want to make you feel guilty. I only want to see you enjoy yourself." His words, while flattering, unnerved her.

"Why?" she snapped. "You don't know me." He watched her, his eyes flickering with a confusion of emotions. "You and I have known each other less than twenty-four hours. You have already spent more money on me than I would have made in a month at the museum. Yet you expect me to just be okay with all of this?"

"I suppose you are right," he said with a sigh. "This sort of situation is very new to me. I haven't a clue how to court a woman."

"And there's that, too." Lily dropped the menu to the table. "You're proper and refined...almost like you're an artifact in one of your cases. And your language borders on archaic." She took a sip from the water glass to steady her nerves, and cleared her throat. "How old are you, anyway?"

Naturally, the waiter chose that moment to appear and demand an order. Lily hadn't even given the menu more than a cursory glance, and Rowan was ready with his order before the kid had his pen poised. She glanced down, and hoping she'd read it right, ordered a club sandwich. The skinny kid looked down his nose at her, but said nothing as he snatched her menu from her hand and skulked away toward the kitchen.

"So?" Lily prodded when they lapsed into silence. Rowan sighed.

"I do wish you had not asked that."

"So you are older than you look."

He hesitated a moment, eyeing her with a careful mask in place. "Considerably."

She swallowed the sick feeling and leveled him with her gaze. "How old?" He glanced around, looking at the empty tables surrounding them and leaned across the table. Lily didn't like that… Nothing good ever came from a man leaning over a table to whisper something to a woman.

"I was born in the winter of 1368, in a small town just outside of Vienna." The accent was Austrian. That answered one question, but left her with ten more, all bubbling up at the same time.

"You're telling me you're almost six-hundred fifty years old years old?" The rational part of her brain flat-lined as the absurdity of the statement overpowered her good sense. "You actually expect me to believe that?"

"Honestly, no. I expect you to believe nothing at this point, except that you are special to me."

"Why?"

"I wish I had an answer for you."

Their food arrived and they ate in silence, Lily picking at her food rather than devouring it as she had originally planned. Something about finding out her lover-slash-personal monster was nearly seven hundred years old had killed her appetite.

He paid the bill and led her back to the car, still without speaking. Once they were back in the relative confinement of the car, Lily turned to him.

"Where are we going now?"

"To check on your car," he said. "It was supposed to be ready an hour ago." She looked at the dash-clock, surprised to find she'd lost almost a whole day in his company.

"Oh, right," she said. "I guess I should be getting home." A glimmer of sadness tumbled through her mind. If it weren't for such a horrible secret, he'd be the perfect man.

The little office was dingy, as most auto shops were, and very stuffy. Rowan's massive frame took up much of the little room, and Lily leaned against the windows to escape his orbit. His large hand crashed down on the bell on the counter, and the sound echoed off the walls. A window facing the garage slid open, and a grease-covered mechanic stuck his head through.

"Rowan," the grease-monkey cheered, "good to see you! Listen, man, I'm sorry, but that car ain't ready." Lily's heart did a backflip. She was stuck. Again. "Had to order a pump, sensor, and a coupl'a valves. Should be ready tomorrow afternoon." She collapsed into the single office chair with a heavy sigh and cradled her head in her hands. The gods seemed to be working against her. She wanted to escape this hell, yet was still forced to rely on Rowan's generosity and hope it wasn't a mistake. It didn't help that her heart told her one thing while her mind screamed something else.

"I am sorry, Lily," he said, and knelt in front of her. He was so warm that his presence was stifling in the little room.

"So, I'm stuck." A deep chuckle rumbled through his chest. Lily clamped down on both her anger and her desire as best she could. "It's not funny."

"Actually, it is. Come on." He took her hand and pulled her out of the chair. Despite the day's unseasonable warmth, the breeze on Lily's skin was cool and refreshing as they left the cramped little office. She took a deep breath and the corners of her mouth curled up in a small, satisfied smile.

"Where are we going now?"

"I assume you would like to go home," he said, and she easily picked up the note of sadness in his voice. "But I can take you anywhere you like."

"Home is good," she replied, and gave him the address. She was surprised by her own disappointment that he hadn't offered to take her back to his house.

Like it or not, she was starting to grow attached to him. How the hell was she supposed to explain that the one and only place she wanted to go was back to his bed, monster or not?

The drive was long and silent. More than once, Rowan caught her watching him, but said nothing. He wanted to quiz her; to find out what she was thinking and if he had any chance at all of winning her affections. He'd been tempted to lure her back to his home by way of his gallery, but thought better of it. Bribery didn't seem to work on this one the way it would on so many others. She'd already trusted him enough to give him one more day, and he did not want to lose what little footing he still had. Nonetheless, he couldn't help but wonder at the look of heartbreak in her eyes.

Amazingly, the problem of the old god had not once crossed his mind as he treated her to a day seeing the Savannah sights. As the haunting memory of Loki's demands filtered through his mind, his mood darkened considerably. She would notice, too, because she was perceptive. Rowan had to clear his thoughts.

He focused on the scenery as they left the city and moved into a more suburban, almost rural, setting.

He'd never been anywhere near her little community, even on his longer runs. He'd never had a reason. As they entered her neighborhood, he noticed that it was a beautiful area, and her small house backed up to the woods leading away from town. He pulled the car into her driveway, and a plan started to form in his mind. She definitely had a sense of adventure... He only hoped she was the outdoor type.

Lily's mind was a whirl of thoughts as he helped her out of the car and gathered the purchases. The bags alone told how much money he'd spent on her, and the thought turned her stomach. She had nothing to give him in return.

Except...

The attraction was undeniable, but also inconvenient and more than a little frustrating. She'd never wanted someone the way she wanted him, but she'd also never been faced with the reality of someone not entirely human. Or willing to spend exorbitant amounts of money on her. That made her more uncomfortable than anything else.

She spent the entire ride home agonizing over how to get him into her home, while simultaneously questioning the whole idea of wanting him there in the first place. But when he took the decision from her by leading the way to her front door, she sighed with relief...only to be immediately flooded with worry that her home wouldn't be up to his standards.

"This is cozy," he commented of her small living room, again removing the fear. "It feels like coming home."

What the hell?

"Uh, thanks," Lily muttered, and squeezed past him to drop her purse on the coffee table. "Want a drink or something?"

"Thank you, but no. I was thinking perhaps we might take a walk together." Lily brightened.

"I'd like that," she replied, and started toward the back of the house. "Just let me change my shoes."

CHAPTER SIX

Closing her bedroom door, Lily fell against it in a heap. Conflicting emotions again nagged at her, leaving her torn between wanting him to follow and needing a moment to recover. The concept of him having a second nature was a distant and vague problem. She had a much more immediate problem; she needed to deal with her stuttering heart and butterfly-filled stomach. Why his being so close had such an effect on her was so strange, but she liked it. She couldn't remember the last time she'd enjoyed a man's company so much.

Hell, she couldn't remember the last time she'd had a man's company.

Lily slipped off her sandals and pulled her sneakers out from under the bed. Her shaking hands made it impossible to tie them, so she threw them to the floor and stalked into the bathroom to splash cool water on her face. Despite the repeated tries to calm herself, Lily couldn't forget about the pressing problem. A large shape-shifter wandering around her house, waiting to go for a walk. She just hoped he had more on the agenda than a walk, and felt the flush of embarrassment for daring to hope. Lily thrust her feet into her shoes, wrangled her hands into submission, and laced them a little too tightly.

By the time she left the bedroom, Rowan had already found and disappeared into the yard. A thrill of anticipation shivered into the pit of her stomach at the sight of his broad shoulders blocking her back door. He was a massive man, and in his arms she felt small and safe.

The wounds on her hips ached in response, but she pushed the pain to the back of her mind and skipped down the hall toward him.

"Just promise you aren't taking me out into the woods to kill me," she joked, and squeezed past him to sprint across the yard. He chuckled, and the deep, throaty sound tied her insides in knots.

"I have no intention of harming you, Lily." He closed the distance in three long strides, and clasped her tiny hand in his large one. Together they walked deep into the woods, conversation often idling in favor of taking in the beauty of their surroundings. Several times Lily heard Rowan breathe deeply through his nose, his chest expanding with each breath. More than once she had to stop herself from reaching out to touch him. She wanted to…badly. But she wouldn't. She was still a little afraid of him, and of this thing growing between them.

"So how does this shifter thing work?" she asked as they crossed a small creek.

"What do you mean?"

"You're over six hundred years old… How long will you live?"

She caught the ghost of a smile on his lips. "Until I find my mate." She pulled him to a stop and turned to stare at him with one eyebrow raised.

"Really? Like magic or something? You just know you've found your mate and that allows you to stop living?"

"Not exactly," he replied, his eyes picking up a sparkle that mocked her. She wanted to smack him. And kiss him. And smack him. But mostly, kiss him.

"Then do tell. I can't exist another second without you telling me." She snorted, and the laughter broke out of him. Rowan tugged her hand, pulling her hard against his chest, and wrapped his arms around her. Lily nearly suffocated against his chest and she hardly noticed for every nerve in her body firing at his sudden nearness.

"I will tell you anything you want to know," he replied as he let her go. "Let us keep walking and I shall explain."

"Okay…" she muttered, stepping away.

"I think better when I am on the move."

"Understandable." She swallowed hard, trying to push down the desire to crawl back up against him. "Tell me."

Rowan took her hand again and tugged her forward. Lily glanced up at the sky, surprised by the clouds forming above the trees. The day had been so warm and so pleasant that she hated to see it ruined by an evening storm that could bring in more cold, dreary weather.

"My kind have quite a shelf-life," he said after a moment's thought.

"So I gathered," she replied with a smirk. Rowan cut his eyes at her.

"I think the oldest unmated shifter recorded lived over four thousand years. She never mated because she enjoyed the feeling of immortality. The last time she was seen was not long after I was born. No one really knows if she died, or simply shifted to exist in animal form."

"Okay," Lily said. The whole thing sounded like some strange fairy tale. Though she'd seen him mid-shift, her mind still couldn't process it as the truth.

"When we mate, part of what makes us who we are is transferred to the other. I suppose you could call it magic... Many cultures do."

"You know this sounds insane, right?"

"I know. But to fully understand me, you need to know this." Fighting the urge to laugh, Lily motioned with her hand for him to continue. "Mating, for my kind, is more than just sex. More than a simple commitment. There is what I suppose you would call a ritual." He fixed her with a hard gaze. "Not to be taken lightly by either."

"I understand," she said, her voice barely above a whisper from the intensity of his gaze.

"When I mate, part of my soul will transfer to my woman, thereby extending her life and allowing mine to end." She stared at him, her mind blank, yet teeming with this new information. The only way to reconcile it was to listen as if he were telling her fiction. If and when the time came, she would face reality. But not here, out in the woods alone with him. "When my mate passes to the next life, I will follow."

"Wow."

"What?"

"It's so romantically tragic," she said, lost for anything else to fill the void. Rowan's hard stare softened, and a lopsided smile took over one side of his face.

"It is. But after almost six hundred and fifty years in this life, it would be a welcome tragedy."

"Are you saying you want to die?"

"Not at all," he corrected, squeezing her hand for emphasis, "but the ability to lead a quasi-normal life is intriguing." He tugged her forward again, pulling her deeper into the woods. In the distance, the sound of rushing water blotted out the quiet of the forest. Lily knew there were falls in the woods, but she'd never been so far out before. But even that wasn't enough to distract her from the thousand questions bubbling up in her mind.

"When you mate, do you still shift?"

Rowan smiled at her in the waning light. "We do. Of course, the excitement of a new relationship often triggers the shift, and a new mating can be dangerous for both parties involved."

Lily stumbled, but whether from the shock of the statement or the rotted log under her feet, she didn't know. Rowan's arms were around her, lifting her from her feet before she even realized she was falling. He'd told her earlier that his shift was triggered by sleeping with her... Did that mean something? Was she meant to be his mate? Her insides did a summersault.

"Are you well?" he asked, steadying her.

"I'm fine..." she lied. She was as far from fine as a person could get without being in a padded room.

"You do not look fine."

"I'm all right, I promise."

"I don't believe you." Lily tried to pull back and stand on her own, but his arms were firm and unmoving around her. One big hand brushed across her cheek and neck to rest under her hair. Lily's head fell back and she looked up at his sparkling blue eyes, again feeling that pang of jealousy at the thick eyelashes surrounding them. "If you were all right you wouldn't be shaking the way you are."

She was shaking, but not from fear. Anticipation overrode every other emotion, and she leaned toward him, seeking his mouth. Rowan bent his head, just out of her reach, and smiled. He brushed his lips across hers softly, and Lily sighed with relief. He pulled her tighter against him, lifting her to her toes, and slanted his mouth across hers, drawing her breath into him as his tongue dipped and twined against hers.

Just as fast, he backed away, holding her at arm's length. "How well do you know these woods?" he asked with lunatic glee as the light in the trees took on Rowan and the pink tones of an evening storm. Lily froze, the reality of her situation rushing into her mind.

"Oh, my God," she gasped, pulling away from him and backing away. "You did bring me out here to kill me!"

"No," Rowan howled, panic crawling into his features, "I simply asked is all."

Lily wasn't convinced, even when her back hit a tree. She hesitated. "Pretty well…" she said, trailing off into a pause.

"Could you find your way back on your own?"

"Yes…" she drew the word out over a whole breath. He smiled, but the humor was gone. His handsome face looked feral. She didn't like it at all.

"Good," he said. "I want to play a game."

"Are you insane?" she shrieked, stumbling back over the tree's roots to hide behind it. Not that it would protect her should he decide to attack.

"Perhaps." Rowan reached for his collar, one by one tugging the buttons loose. Lily's mouth watered at the sight of his tattoo-streaked chest coming into view. "Before you and I can make any decisions about what this relationship is or is not, you need to see the truth." So he was planning on mating with her. His shirt fluttered to the ground, and Lily had a very hard time concentrating on his words. All she wanted was to trace the lines of ink with her tongue. "You need to see me for who and what I am." His shoes came off into his hands and thumped to the ground, leaving his feet bare. Even his toes elicited a reaction from her aching body. When he reached for his belt, Lily bit her knuckles and pressed her face against the cool wood of the tree to stifle a moan. Rowan smiled. "And then you and I will play a little game of hide and seek."

One by one he popped the buttons on the fly of his jeans. Lily's mouth went dry in anticipation of what was hiding beneath. The game she could handle so long as she got to look at—and eventually touch— that glorious body.

"What...what are the stakes?" she asked in a cracked voice.

"You get back to your house first, and I leave you alone."

"And if you catch me?"

"Then I have you." Her stomach did a flip and every nerve in her body sang with excitement. She'd gladly throw the competition for another tumble with him. "There is a catch..." he trailed off, and stepped out of his jeans. Tattoos ran over his hips and curled down his thighs and calves, drawing her gaze to the apex of his thighs where he displayed a proud erection *Anything,* she thought, *to have him again.* "You must witness my change."

Wait, what?

Dread flooded her chest. All sense of desire vanished as she stared at him. This game didn't seem like so much fun anymore. When it was in the past, she could handle his second nature…but to face it, to be hunted by it, was more than she could stand.

"Do not fear me, Lily," he said as the air around him began to shimmer. "I swear you are safe with me." His voice took on a second timbre, as if passing through two sets of vocal chords. "I will never hurt you." She watched in horror as his fingers elongated and his fingernails split the skin, warping into the talons she'd seen earlier. His face shifted, the muscle and bone beneath his skin twisting and pulling and stretching. Within seconds, the change was complete. Standing before her was a large, stocky wolf, covered with a thick, silver coat with black marks twisting through it. Other than the tattoo-like patterns, only the intelligent blue-and-gold eyes remained of the man she knew.

Lily bit back a scream and turned to run. A laughing bark followed her into the trees, clenching her heart in a fist of terror. She ran like the wind, leaping over downed trees and dodging low branches in her race to get back to her house. Her ears searched for footfalls behind her, but heard none. The smell of rain hung heavy in the air, and humidity crowded her lungs, making it hard to breathe. She dragged in a deep breath and turned to the left, cutting towards what should be her nearest neighbor's yard. If he were following, it would be too obvious to go straight home, and as the monster he was he would overtake her without a problem.

Her breath came in harsh, heavy gasps and despite the demands of her mind to run faster, she found herself slowing, her goal growing more and more distant. Her legs grew weak and rubbery, and every sound echoed as her fear-stricken mind told her he was right behind her.

She should have been back to the house by now. Had she turned the wrong way? Was she so distracted by his presence that she didn't realize how far out he'd taken her? Panic rose with each beat of her heart, with each sluggish footstep. What felt like a hand reached out for her ankle, stalling her progress forward.

Lily gasped and collapsed to the forest floor. She knew he was toying with her, as any predator was wont to do with its prey. It was dark now, and the moon was only visible in slivers between the clouds and the cracks in the canopy. In the distance, lightning brightened the backs of the clouds. He should have found her long ago. Her legs were too tired to carry her, her body too fatigued from the night before. Still, she shoved herself up and trudged on. Only, nothing was familiar now. It could have been the exhaustion, but Lily knew better. She knew she'd gotten herself lost in the woods.

With a monster.

She shoved away from a tree and sprinted forward. Her second wind hit. The endorphins kicked in and she ran with renewed vigor back the way she came with the single intention of getting home and locking the doors. She turned when she thought she recognized something, and within moments, house lights could be seen winking between the trees. The lightning was growing closer, and followed by small, angry rumbles of thunder. Nearby, a wolf howled, the sound like a hunter's cry to her tired mind, and that was the point when Lily knew she wasn't going to make it home.

Terror-stricken, she pushed herself to the absolute limit. Her body ached, her legs like rubber encased in skin, and her head pounding with the exertion. The brightly burning porch lights beckoned to her, calling her forward into their safely welcoming glow, but her feet tangled in the underbrush and Lily tumbled to the ground. The dust of decomposed brush fluttered up around her face as she went down, gathering in her weary lungs and causing a series of hard, painful sneezes. She covered her face with her hands and tried to stop them, but the expulsion of dust from her body was adamant.

Lily tried to push up from the ground but her arms refused to work. Even if they had, she doubted her aching legs would support her weight, even to break the tree-line and find her back porch. It was close… close enough that she could see the neighborhood, see her safety. But her body revolted, refusing to give in and let her push like she had before. Her energy spent, she could do little more than lie in the dirt and wait to either recover or be caught.

Through the keen, monochrome eyes of the wolf, the small sliver of Rowan's human consciousness watched the poor girl on the ground. She struggled to breathe, to sit up, to simply stay conscious. One nature dueled with the other, a battle of cunning versus determination. The animal—the dominant thought process—wanted to pounce, to take her hard and fast and without consideration, but that single shred of human emotion fought valiantly, peeling at the layers of selfish need as she struggled to her hands and knees to crawl forward.

Despite the fun both parts had at the game, it was time to bring it to an end. To let Lily face him and make her decisions.

Slowly, her strength returned and she was able to slither to her knees. Still unsure as to whether she would be able to walk, she leaned over and shuffled forward on hands and knees, gaining precious inches, but it wasn't enough. When she heard the thunder of paws on the ground, she knew it was already too late.

Large, silver legs came down on either side of her face, and the heat of his body washed over her. Lily's heart hammered in her chest, pounding her ribs into the ground. Her belly flooded with warmth when the animal snuffled at her, its damp breath skittering across her neck. Around her, the air shimmered and she felt his weight shift behind her. Rowan's human lips, wet and warm, grazed her ear and the crackling of his hands and arms returning to their natural shape made her stomach hurt. She squeezed her eyes closed and waited for the transformation to be over.

"Caught you," he breathed, catching her earlobe between his teeth. His bare chest pushed down against her sweat-soaked back, sticking the cold, wet fabric of the T-shirt to her skin. "You know what that means." Heat coursed through her body. Lily shivered, anticipation and fear swirling around each other and spiraling out from the spot where his bottom lip pressed against her neck.

"Yes," she whispered with the last of her breath. Rowan's hands lifted from the dirt and traveled the length of her sides, bunching her shirt into balls beneath his fists.

"Say it," he growled.

"I'm…yours," she conceded. His breath, a wet, hot puff against her neck, stirred the tiny hairs there as he growled in satisfaction. His teeth grazed the corded vein in her neck, nipping lightly at the flesh and making her wince. Even after the horrific sight of his change, Lily still found herself pressing her thighs together to curb the tingling in her sex.

"That is right… Mine," he echoed, and hooked his big hands around her hips. Pain stabbed out from the wounds, and Lily let out a small cry. Rowan seemed to not hear her protest as he pulled her onto her back, and covered her with his body again to prevent her escape. Before she could move, he straddled her legs and his hands landed on her shoulders in a possessive hold. Their eyes locked, and in those large, blue orbs she watched his emotions swirl. He was triumphant, and happy, and…uncertain. His gaze searched hers, as if looking for permission.

Lily surprised herself, reaching up to caress his jaw with her fingertips. The skin was smooth, yet pebbled with a day's stubble and the fine hairs retracting from his coat. He let go a breath she hadn't realized he was holding and his lips came down to brush across hers. They whispered over her forehead and the line of her cheekbone to her ear. Lily whimpered; the sound surprisingly wanton even to her own ears. His body vibrated with silent laughter and his lips tickled along her neck.

His teeth, sharp and smooth, picked at the skin along her shoulder, no doubt leaving marks. The T-shirt she wore ripped, and cool night air rushed over her skin. In the distance, thunder rumbled, but Lily scarcely heard it for the rushing of blood in her ears. The pants she wore went the same way, rent from her body by his insistent hands. She gasped as his feverish fingers slipped over her skin, followed quickly by his lips and tongue.

Lily gasped in surprise as he stilled near her hips, and his lips pressed in a round arch over each of the wounds there. His tongue, rough like sandpaper, dragged across them with a light sting, which he quickly soothed with more small kisses. Her hand sought out his head, fingertips rushing through the growth. Lightning streaked across the sky overhead, followed by a rumble of thunder and the first drops of cold rain on her overheated skin.

Lily sank into the moment, loving the feel of his skin against hers, and moved to draw her hands over his shoulders. Before she could, he growled and flipped her back onto her stomach in the dirt. She grunted as the wind left her lungs, and his big hands clutched at her hips, dragging her back to her knees as he thrust forward and buried himself deep inside her. She screamed, her voice echoing off the trees. The sky split wide, spilling stinging rain onto her bare back. Rowan pulled back and thrust forward again, a sharp, hard push that sent needles of pleasure and pain ripping through her. Thunder cracked overhead and she pressed her forehead to the muddy ground. With each movement he almost completely left her body only to drive home again, jerking at her hips to pull her closer.

Lily could do little more than dig her fingers into the wet earth and moan as he took her, filling her again and again. Rowan bent over her, hips still pounding against her and clutched at her breasts, pinching her nipples and drawing a series of near sobs from her throat.

His big hands were everywhere on her, touching and pulling and pinching as he continued with brutal thrusts. Lightning zagged across the sky, striking a nearby tree with enough force to shake the ground beneath them. The crack of thunder that followed seemed to give him new purpose and he came into her harder, faster, his cock threatening to split her body in two. She pushed back against him with each thrust, gasping his name over and over. His hands curled around her, found her clit, and he pinched the bud of nerves between his thumb and forefinger. The sensation rocketed Lily into orgasm and she screamed as her body contracted around him, begging him deeper, harder. Her whole body trembled with release, but he continued on, grunts and growls of pleasure mixing with the sounds of the storm.

Rowan could have died right at that moment and not regretted a thing. Lily, screaming in orgasm beneath him was the best damn thing he'd ever felt. He wanted to come, to give the last shreds of himself over to her, but he wanted to feel her again. Even as she unwound and her cries slowed to whimpers, he continued his brutal thrusts, holding back his own release to savor the feel of her tight, wet heat surrounding his cock.

He closed his eyes and tipped his head back to the sky, letting the torrential downpour spatter his face. Rowan groaned and pushed forward until his hips met hers with crushing force, Lily's much abused body still spasming with the remnants of orgasm. His balls pulsed impatiently, but he wasn't ready to give in. It was too soon for this ultimate pleasure to be over.

Lily started to crumble beneath him, but he held tightly to her hips, supporting her weight as he thrust with bruising force. She gasped and moaned beneath him, her fingers flexing and digging into the ground with each slap of his tightened testicles against her sex, her body still demanding him deeper and harder.

Rowan's vision went hazy, flickering on the edges as he drove home again and again. He could feel the change threatening on the heels of the orgasm that so begged for release. Under him, her body trembled. Her small, slender fingers danced backwards and locked onto his hip with surprising force, curling into his skin and pulling him forward. Each push drew a whimper from her and even under the pressure of his hands she rocked back to meet his every thrust.

"Rowan..." she gasped, and the sound of his name turned to a moan. Her hand left his hip to snake between her own legs. He felt the pressure of her fingertips against her center and the gentle reshaping of his balls as they bounced against her hand, and it only urged him on. He had to feel her come again, even as his cock threatened to split with the force of impending orgasm, tightening and pulsing in preparation for his release. He forced each labored breath out through his nose, urging his body not to betray him. He could not lose control with her again. He'd already hurt her once; there was no telling what a second change would do to her.

A shrill cry echoed off the trees and she curled beneath him, her inner muscles seizing and clamping tightly around his cock. Rowan couldn't stop this time; he slammed into her with brutal force, driving her down into the mud as the power of his own release threatened to snap the last vestiges of his control. With one final jerk of his hips he came, falling against her and crushing her into the ground as he filled her with his seed.

The animal howl filled his head, and crackling pain raced through his body. Her breathless moan sent him flying from her as the change forced itself on him. With the last shred of human consciousness, he looked down at her tired face.

The starbursts faded from her vision as Lily took mental stock of her body. Everything was still attached. No new wounds. And heavy rain battered her now unprotected body. She lifted her head as she turned over and looked up into the eyes of the same large, silver-and-black wolf that had hunted her only moments before. Its eyes were Rowan's eyes, large, blue, and too human for the animal that bore them. Only that keen stare and the uncanny knowledge that he would relish the chase kept her in her subservient position. Raw terror replaced the post-coital adrenaline, but so long as she focused on his eyes, the urge to flee was manageable.

"Rowan?" she asked, having to yell over the torrential downpour. The animal huffed. "Are you in there?" She was terrified beyond belief, but she'd only moments before had sex with the man inside the beast. She had to face the beast now, because like it or not, she'd grown attached to the man.

Her body ached from the abuse it had taken, and her legs protested as she tried to stand. Both the ground and her body were muddy and she slipped and would have landed face-first had the large, silver head not materialized under her hands to steady her.

Lily's first reaction was repulsion, followed quickly by guilt. As lightning brightened the sky, she spotted two muddy handprints in the middle of his back.

"Oh, no. Rowan, I'm sorry..." she nearly sobbed. "I got you all dirty!" The wolf turned its head to look at her, its intelligent eyes filled with mocking humor. She cringed. "Yeah, I know..." She felt silly all of a sudden. "I'm standing here in the middle of a storm, naked, in the woods with a monster. You're all wet, and I'm muddy. Why should I worry about getting you a little dirty?" The wolf huffed again, bumping its large head against her midsection as his shoulders shook like he was laughing.

Lily shivered. The rainfall was lighter and the lightning a bit less frequent, but her damp skin was cold, gooseflesh rising all over with each gust of wind. Her clothes were in shreds for the second time in twenty-four hours, and she had no idea where she was. Being lost so close to home was not a good feeling, huge lupine protector standing by or not.

"You really need to change back now," she said with chattering teeth. "I'm cold and I don't know my way home in the dark." He whined, a low sound that she barely heard under the patter of rain through the trees. Rowan leaned against her and she sank into his fur. He was so warm, and her teeth clacked together so hard her jaw hurt. He felt feverish…but that could be a side effect of the icy rain and her low tolerance for cold.

He started to walk and Lily followed along, still burrowed down against his side to avoid the rain dripping from the trees. Within moments the house lights came back into view and the welcome sight of her own back door sent Lily sprinting naked toward it. She barreled through the door, leaving the large wolf behind and headed straight for the bathroom. Her next move was toward a very hot shower and lots of soap.

CHAPTER SEVEN

"I see you are still in one piece."

His voice startled her. Lily jumped, knocking her shampoo bottle to the floor. He filled the doorway, his bare body streaked with mud. Again, fear tickled at the back of her mind, but the welcoming steam of the shower called to her with a much stronger voice.

"I need to clean up," she said, at a loss for conversation. "I'm muddy." He watched her with an amused expression.

"So I see." His eyes raked over her and Lily shrank back in embarrassment. "I would take my leave, but I am, quite unfortunately, without clothes."

"We left them in the woods." *Way to be intelligent, Lily,* she berated herself. "Do you want a shower?" She didn't know how she wanted him to respond. The amused smile turned predatory, and her much abused body tightened in anticipation.

"I thought you would never ask." Immediately he was filling the bathroom. Rowan pushed the door closed — to keep the heat in, he explained — and stepped into the shower. Lily stared at the curtain with her mouth agape until he poked his head out and grinned at her. "You coming in?"

She shook herself. "Yeah," she replied, and took his outstretched hand.

Later, they lay across her bed, Rowan taking up the majority of it. She was sprawled across his chest. Lily lay still, listening to the contented purr deep in his chest. She batted thoughts back and forth, trying to decide which emotion would rule. Part of her wanted to fear him for what he was. Part of her wanted to hate him for lying to her. Part was intimidated by his flippant spending of money. But mostly she just wanted to lie in his arms and pretend the rest of the world didn't exist.

"You still awake?" he asked, his voice a deep rumble beneath her ear.

"Mmm..." she responded, and burrowed tighter into his side.

"You do understand that you and I need to talk, correct?"

"Later." Her jaw tightened as the fear leaked back into her brain. For a few moments, she'd been able to turn it all off, and whether he realized it or not he was bringing it all back in a big way. "Or now," she sighed, pushing up on her hands, and spun to sit cross-legged next to him. Her bathrobe gaped at the bottom and she fought to situate it so that she was at least somewhat covered. It would do no good for him to be distracted by her naked body. Rowan sat up as well, leaning back against the headboard to look at her. "Talk," Lily demanded.

"You know now what I am."

"Yes."

"And you know the commitment my kind makes."

"Yes." Lily leaned away and stared at him. "What's your point?"

"I know you and I have known each other only a single day, and I do not want to make unreasonable demands of you, yet…"

"Rowan?" she prodded when he stalled.

"You are my mate, Lily." The sentence was like a pallet of bricks to the chest. He leaned up and Lily stumbled off the bed to put distance between them. "I have known it since the moment I first laid eyes on you. I feel it in my blood, just as I feel my second nature." The connection they shared was strong; she couldn't deny that. But it still felt like a smack across the face. "I am not asking you to make that decision now," he continued. "But I want to always be honest with you."

Lily's back hit the wall just in time to keep her standing. Her jaw worked like she would speak, but she had no voice. Rowan watched her, his keen stare betraying no emotion even as frightened tears stung the corners of hers. Panic bubbled up in her throat as he threw back the blanket covering his body and placed his feet on the floor. She forced her eyes closed against the tempting sight of him.

"I have to tell you that with me comes trouble I dare say you do not want to be involved in."

"Then why did you bother to tell me all this? Why didn't you just walk away and leave it when you could?"

"Because...with you, I cannot control myself," he said. She closed her eyes and sighed. Something in her chest ached. "I can see I have upset you." He levered himself to his feet. "I will leave you to consider the proposition," he said. "I will not bother you until your decision is made." He crossed the room, unashamed by his nudity, and cupped her face in his calloused palm. Rowan gently pressed his lips to her cheekbone. "The decision is yours, and as much as I want to keep you, I will not try to influence you."

Lily remained immobile, listening as he moved through her house. The tinkling of his keys was barely audible above the rush of thoughts through her head and when she heard the front door quietly open and close, she sank to the floor with her head in her hands. The purr of his car's engine flared to life and retreated just as the tears started to fall.

Rowan's vision blurred as he waited for the road to clear. Every thought in his head was insanity, beating against both his senses and his better judgment. He wanted to turn the car around, to go back and demand that Lily accept the inevitable. They were a perfect match. Surely only a true mate could elicit such frenzy from his kind...

No.

He had to control the alpha urges. Lily was a modern woman with a modern mind. She wouldn't be swayed by such barbaric activity. Women like Lily didn't understand his kind. She hadn't known what he was, or how to react to that knowledge.

Plus, there was no way of knowing exactly when his past—long-forgotten as it may seem—would catch up with him again. With his track record, his best guess was not long.

Yes, Lily would be the perfect leverage against him should Loki discover the relationship. And she would be the perfect victim should he decide to exact any sort of revenge. Loki never needed a reason to act, but given one the retribution would be absolute. Rowan could not stand the thought of having her death on his conscience, because death it certainly would be.

Rowan pulled onto the highway and turned his windshield wipers against the light rain misting the road. He had to go home and wait it out. No matter what he wanted, the decision had to be hers. Besides, in the event that she agreed, he needed to do some research. He had no idea of the mechanics of a mating—he'd attended a ceremony or two, but by then the true mating was done. To see a mating in its entirety was unheard of. He'd heard the stories of his parents, and now his kind was increasingly rare.

Frustrated, he turned on the radio and found something loud and angry. Patience was a virtue he sorely needed to learn. If he couldn't give her the space to choose him fairly, how could he ever expect to grow old with her?

Lily cried herself to sleep that night, and woke the next morning with swollen, sleep-crusted eyes. Despite the drama and the fact that she'd only known Rowan two days, she missed him. His big, warm body by her side had been an unexpected comfort. Without him, her queen-size bed seemed cold and lonely.

She was still absolutely terrified of him—not of the man, but of the creature lurking beneath his skin. The animal that had hunted and caught her. That had pinned her to the ground and taken her in the most primal of ways. That purred like a kitten when he held her. Though she'd witnessed the shift with her own eyes, Lily still couldn't reconcile the man with the monster.

She paced between her living room and kitchen, alternating pulling her hair with teary sniffles. The clothes he bought her were still carefully wrapped and waiting for her to open them. The bags rested on her couch, and the inordinate amount of money contained within made her stomach turn. Rowan hadn't thought twice about the purchases, and that knowledge only made her feel more rotten.

Why couldn't she just accept him and be happy to follow through with this foolhardy plan?

Because it was just that: foolhardy.

She didn't know him. Didn't have a clue how he lived or if she would be in danger from him. He said something about trouble already—so there was one huge red flag. Plus, he'd already demonstrated an inability to control the shift around her. Again, she'd seen that firsthand. But she'd also seen his beautiful blue eyes encased in the face of the wolf, and recognized how the tribal patterns inked into his skin bled into his fur.

With a growl, Lily threw herself into her computer chair and typed the word "shapeshifter" into the search engine. To her astonishment, thousands of results came up, including a ridiculous article on

Wikipedia, and something called *The Shapeshifter Codex* which absolutely blew her mind.

> Throughout historical and modern folklore, shape shifters have been consistently painted as monsters. From the pure-breed shifters to the mutated Lycanthropes, all two-natured have been given a bad name. What popular culture fails to mention is that all breeds of shifter are inherently human, most having developed extra chromosomes, much like the mutations seen in Stan Lee's "X-Men" comics. As such, shifters retain human thought even while shifted or during lunar frenzy. Many legends dictate that shape shifters are descended from gods, the second nature a mere byproduct of divine blood.

The site had obviously been compiled by a folklore enthusiast, and detailed every aspect of a shifter's existence, starting with the most general "what kind of shifter are you?" and ending in the minutiae of eye shape and hair growth with respect to the shifter's nature. The amount of information was mind-boggling, and Lily had no way of processing it all. She was ready to throw her hands up and close the site down when a link nestled into the text caught her attention.

Mating Rituals

A nervous lump crawled into her throat as the mouse hovered over the words. She inhaled sharply and clicked on it.

The next page contained two subjects: *Lycanthrope* and *Natural Shifter*. She followed the second link and was rewarded with a list of animal types with the header Natural Shift Familiar Form. Lily was already numb as she selected "wolf" from the list.

At the top of the next page was a photograph of a tawny and black wolf, sleek and feminine, standing next to a human male that appeared to be in his mid-thirties.

> *Mating, the most sacred ceremony of a shifter's existence, remains shrouded in mystery.*

Lily stared at the page in shock. Some yahoo was taking this stuff way too seriously. Probably that proposed folklore nut with one too many lattes in his blood stream. But...

No, she wasn't going to play the what-if game and get bogged down in details. In the light of morning her game of hide and seek with Rowan seemed more like a strange dream, and it was easier to discount everything on this site. If she followed that train of thought, she'd have to let herself believe that the supernatural was real and that the man she'd just spent two nights screwing seven ways from Sunday embodied all of it.

An unfortunate casualty, she thought with a sigh and backed through the site to the main page. If only he were normal, she could easily see herself fitting into his life. Being the kept woman of a wealthy, good-looking man wasn't such a bad thing.

You are my mate, Lily…

A ripple of lust shivered through her belly as her throat simultaneously tightened. How the hell could she want someone so much and still fear him? She growled and slapped at her mouse to clear the screen-saver, and the phone rang. She darted across the room and snatched it up on the second ring.

"Hello?"

"Lily Redway?"

"Yes."

"This is Carolyn Reynolds at the Collins-Goodwin Gallery." The Gallery… She'd worked for one of its subsidiaries until the museum closed. Lily swallowed the lump in her throat and listened. "A temporary contract position with an immediate start date has become available. The owner of the collection has specifically requested you based on your resume and qualifications. I've taken the liberty of scheduling an interview for you this morning at eleven-thirty."

"Wow…" she breathed into the phone. This was a surprise and greatly unexpected, too.

"I will see you at eleven-thirty, Miss Redway." The telephone clicked in her hand, and the line went dead. So much for being given a choice…but if Carolyn Reynolds was anything like Lily had heard, courteous closings had no place in her efficient lifestyle.

Shaking her head, Lily turned her attention back to her monitor, only halfway paying attention to the words there. There was too much going on… too many things happening at once, and not enough thought processes available to make them all make sense. She picked up her coffee cup and took a long drink as she continued to read.

Tribal Markings

Every pure-breed shifter carries markings, which not only signify his or her original clan, but can give an inkling of true age. The markings often appear as tattoos, which spread with age, and remain visible even when in animal form.

Lily thought about the fluid, intricate lines crisscrossing the majority of Rowan's body, and shuddered. Thin tendrils reached toward his face, one of the only unmarred areas of skin on him. If the passage was correct, he in truth could be well over six-hundred years old. And the way each black line curved over his skin, the way the thinnest of those lines reached out above his ear toward his eye…

Growling, Lily closed the website down and punched the monitor off. It would do no good to remain on the topic of his body…of Rowan at all. She had to get a grip on herself, and do it fast.

She was all too ready to move on when a knock at her front door startled her into nearly dropping her coffee cup. Muttering curses under her breath and smacking at the drops of brown liquid staining her nightgown, she stalked across the room and snatched open the door. The receptionist from Rowan's office stood there, holding in one hand the keys to her car, and in the other a clipboard.

"Sign this," Lurch said in the same curt, efficient manner he'd used at her interview, and thrust the form into her hands. It was a release for the keys.

"Um, thank you," she said as he dropped the keys into her hand and stalked away without another word. Standing in her robe on her doorstep, Lily looked at the ring of keys then at her car in the driveway and sighed. Disappointed that Rowan hadn't brought them herself, she gave herself a sharp mental slap. Wanting him and doing the best thing for herself seemed at this point to be polar opposites. He exuded danger. And mystery. She mentally slapped herself again. It was much easier to ignore his second nature when she was in the room with him but then again, he'd said he would let her make the decision. And sadly, as she looked across her front yard and down the street at her quiet neighborhood, she knew that her answer would have to be no.

With time and persuasion it could be something different, but without his presence the odds weren't good that she would get the persuasion she so desperately wanted.

"I'm so sorry I'm late," Lily gasped as she rushed through the door of the office. "There was an accident and I didn't have the phone number."

"That's quite all right," the receptionist said brightly. "Miss Reynolds will see you now." She stood with a perky pop to her shoulders that made Lily want to retch. "This way."

She exhaled a deep sigh and tucked a wayward strand of hair back into her ponytail. Lily hated feeling so unsteady, but truth be told she'd been so busy feeling sorry for herself that she'd nearly forgotten the appointment only an hour later. She remembered at the last possible second and thrown herself together, running out of the house like her rear was on fire.

The receptionist led her to an austere office, decorated in clean lines with little in the way of nonfunctional furniture. *Not at all like Rowan's building*, she thought, and mentally kicked herself again. It seemed to be a running theme.

The room might be cold, but it felt safe.

"Lily Redway," the woman behind the desk— who, with her school-marm chignon, coldly matched the room—said as she stood and extended her hand. "I am Carolyn Reynolds."

"A pleasure."

"Have a seat." Despite her looks and efficient speech, she seemed friendly enough. Lily sat stiffly on the chair, a thin smile straining her face. "I am sure you understand that this job is a temporary contract. One of the Gallery's benefactors needs a curator for his private collection, which must be cataloged and cased for a two-month show to begin in exactly four weeks." Lily felt sick. Her throat tightened and her heart thumped like it had lead weights in it. Surely it couldn't be… "Loren Eshu asked for only the best," Carolyn said, and Lily's body unlocked gratefully. It wasn't Rowan. But…

"Loren? Since when does he have a collection?"

Carolyn raised one neatly manicured eyebrow. "You know him?"

"I do… He was a member and donor at the Gallery. I knew he was an art lover, but I never would have imagined him the type to want a private show."

"He has a highly impressive collection, and quite frankly, Lily, you are the only plausible candidate I have. Can you start tomorrow?"

Lily closed her eyes and took a deep, calming breath. Little by little she pulled her thoughts together. Of course it wasn't Rowan. Those sorts of coincidences didn't happen to people like her, and Carolyn seemed like the last woman on earth to keep company with a man like Rowan. At least Loren would be a familiar face. Not the job opportunity of a lifetime, but those only came along once in a lifetime…and she already passed hers up.

"Of course," she said calmly. "I'd love to."

"I understand the collection is in disarray, and that quite a bit of it may require restoration, but I am certain you can handle it." Kudos. Awesome. Warm fuzzies spread through Lily from the praise of the woman she'd met in person only ten minutes earlier. She knew the name of course…Carolyn had been the one to sign the papers terminating her previous job.

"I can," Lily assured her. Maybe this job would help prove that the closing of the other gallery was premature. "I enjoy a good challenge." The icy woman cracked a small, brittle smile in response, and Lily knew when Carolyn turned her attention to the computer that she was dismissed.

"Tina will give you the information." Carolyn's attention then focused on the papers in her hand. They were done, and the door behind her cracked open quietly.

"Thank you," Lily said, backing out of the room, and received no response.

Lily's mood on the drive out of town was one of utter confusion. She found herself ecstatic over the job, but beneath the happiness was a hard ache. She missed Rowan, and that reaction alone disturbed her. She'd never had such a reaction to someone before, never craved contact like she did with him. She suspected she was in trouble the first time she saw him. Then he had essentially proposed after forty-eight hours. It wasn't that Lily was afraid of commitment…she was afraid of that sort of commitment. Too fast. Too overwhelming.

She might have had a chance of putting the thoughts out of her head, but a traffic detour took her past his home, where he was leaning out a second-floor window. Shirtless.

Lily winced, jerked her wandering gaze back to the road, and prayed he hadn't seen her. If he tried to contact her—she glanced at her cell phone lying on the seat next to her—it would be over. Luckily—or unluckily, depending on how she looked at it—it never rang and she escaped the city limits with her dignity intact.

But not her heart.

She wanted him in the most primal of ways—as any woman would want a gorgeous man—and without the animal in front of her she found herself believing it all just so she could have him.

"You've lost it, Lily," she told herself, and turned the radio up as she pulled onto the highway. The newscasters had taken over her favorite station again, this time talking about something that seemed totally unreal. "You really have lost it, girl," she said out loud as she listened to the reports of black panther sightings in the area.

"Well, Bob, I never thought I'd hear of panthers in this area."

"Too right, Stacey," Bob laughed. "The last time panthers came to this area, they went home with their tails between their legs."

Stacey groaned. "Bad sports analogy, Bob." Lily echoed the sound and punched the radio button to turn it off. The past forty-eight hours were full of weirdness...the last thing she needed was to look out her back door and think she was staring into the eyes of an African jungle cat.

Rowan spotted the little car long before it reached the street in front of him. Just the glimpse of her face through the windshield—conflicted as it was—made his heart do a back flip. She saw him, of that he was certain, and beyond his vision he could feel her moving closer, like she was already in his blood. The compelling need to meet her at the door overtook him, but he remained rooted to the balcony with every shred of determination he possessed. Rightly so, as she continued past and he realized his wishful thinking would get him nowhere.

CHAPTER EIGHT

To be prepared for Loren Eshu's collection would have meant being prepared for Loren himself. Lily remembered him well. He was friendly enough but in a reserved, cool way that was so different than Rowan's open warmth...and his looks were a stark contrast. Where Rowan was tall, fair, and broad, Loren was smooth and slender, with little definition beneath his silk shirt. His hair was shaggy and black, but gelled back into place, and his angular face clean shaven. His brown eyes sparkled with wickedness. He was roguishly attractive, but something about him kindled a spark of reluctance in her.

Intimidating was the first word that came to mind when she looked at him. He was frightening, but not in an obvious manner. Loren had a fierce look about him; dangerous. His features betrayed a sly insanity, and she knew that behind his lips lay a sharp tongue. But the charming smile on his face dazzled the thoughts right out of her head.

Lily stumbled around awkward reintroductions, following his lead while trying to ignore the curious way he watched her. She then followed him through his home into what looked like a ballroom. Artifact cases lined the walls, stuffed so tightly with items that she could scarcely make out what was in each. They were surrounded by stacks of boxes, each marked with a different symbol. She recognized none of them. It also looked as if he had just moved in.

Loren's collection, while vast, was an epic disaster. Like Rowan's collection, it was filled with unique and bizarre artifacts, but it was not clean and organized. Also unlike Rowan, she realized as she glanced around that the majority of visible pieces were weaponry.

"My grandfather was a war buff," he said to her questioning gaze.

"Interesting." She lifted a spiked flail from a musty box. "If he loved these things so much, why didn't he take better care of them?"

"He did… I'm afraid they've been shuffled from place to place since his passing, and I haven't had much time to give them the love they need." He looked her up and down, and Lily suppressed the urge to shudder. "Which is precisely why I've hired you."

"Well, you probably should have hired a restoration crew first… Some of this stuff is going to need professional care."

"I am sure," he said, crowding her personal space past the point of comfort or propriety, "you are more than capable of handling my things, Lily." The Loren she remembered was not this forward. The way his dark gaze slithered over her skin made her nervous, and she struggled with the urge to run from the room. The double entendre also seemed out of character for him. "I can't for the life of me understand why such a beautiful woman would confine herself to stacks like these."

"It's a living," she replied, tucking a wayward strand of hair behind her ear and turning away from him, "and I love the history." She couldn't look at him anymore. It was too odd, and Rowan's leaving was still too fresh in her mind. *He didn't leave... I didn't call him*, she told herself, but that only made the separation hurt more. "I have to admit, my specialty is more of the oil and watercolor nature," she said, still forcing her hair behind her ears as she paced across the room, "but I think I can handle this."

"Your husband is a lucky man," he said coolly. Lily paused, tension tightening her shoulders and back.

"I'm not married," she offered with great reluctance.

"Boyfriend?"

She paused; refused to look at him. "I was seeing someone."

"Was?"

"Past tense."

"A shame. He doesn't know what he had."

How the hell could he know that? She'd known Loren Eshu in more than just a casual way for a grand total of an hour. Of course, she'd only known Rowan a few hours before she'd crawled into bed with him...and look where that got her. Her luck with rich eccentrics seemed to have run aground. However, she wasn't going to make that mistake again, no matter how charming this man might be.

Still, Loren tried and Lily continued to gently rebuff his advances, citing that recent split. It wasn't entirely false...she had decided not to contact Rowan. His...problems...were a little too much for her to deal with, she told herself. Of course, the more she thought about it the more like a strange dream it all seemed. Plus, she felt the driving need to prove herself as professional to her new, albeit temporary, boss without the possibility of padding her résumé with his affections.

Lily threw herself into her work with a grateful vigor that surprised everyone around her. She liked having something to do—it kept her from thinking too much about...certain people. Plus, having the steady predictability of cataloging a collection gave her distraction from the fact that in the three years she'd lived in Savannah she had yet to secure more than passing acquaintances, and from the constant focus of Loren, who, to her dismay, never left the room, watched her with unnerving interest, and who appeared to greatly enjoy making her squirm.

Planting the millipede under her purse was evil. She was certain he knew it when he did it, but he seemed so delighted by her shriek that he was absolutely unrepentant when she rounded on him and unleashed a tirade that rivaled the fury of Hell. He simply draped one arm around her shoulders, squeezed her, and told her he'd never spring another millipede on her again. He leaned in like he would kiss her forehead, but she quickly ducked out of his grasp and stuffed her head into one of the many boxes.

It wasn't that he was unattractive. He just…well, he was her boss first and foremost, and she reminded herself every time the thought cropped up. He was her employer, and she had a job to do. And her heart simply wasn't ready for another…

Correction.

A relationship. Not another. A relationship.

Growling, Lily flung her notebook to the table and thrust her hands into her hair. Every single thought in her head always circled back around to Rowan-freaking-Keir. Even Loren's collection took her back to him.

"Is there a problem?" Loren's voice cut through the silence, its sarcastic edge tearing at her already raw nerves. Lily pasted a smile on her face and turned to him.

"No...not really," she lied, and wiped her hands on her jeans. "Only that you have a massive collection in horrible shape and your constant hovering is making me nuts."

The bastard laughed at her. "Forgive me for being interested in the future of my collection," he replied with an amused snort. She scowled at him. "Of course, the future of my collection could be much more secure if..." Lily held up a hand to stop him.

"I appreciate the flattery, but I do prefer to work alone," she said, trying hard not to be short with him.

"I was only going to say that it would be more secure if my temporary employee would agree to migrate to my full-time payroll." Her blue eyes snapped up to meet his dark, nearly black ones, and her jaw felt like a broken hinge.

"Full-time?" she stammered. "Like, permanent?"

"Of course. Granted, I am certain I could come up with a list of perks that might make the job seem more worthwhile." She didn't like the way his features curled, or how his whole demeanor became dark and possessive.

"L-let me think about it," she replied, and shrank back toward her work. "And I do work much better undisturbed."

Even after the rebuff he continued to smile. "I will take the hint," he said, and backed away, "for now."

Lily snorted and turned back to the table and her laptop, trying to appear calm and collected despite the chill settling in her stomach. As he left the room, she realized that the work before her was not complex enough to keep her imagination entirely busy.

The similarities between Loren's collection and Rowan's played heavily on her mind. Both contained artifacts thought to be lost to history, and spanned centuries. She wondered briefly if they'd been collected in the same manner...

That was ridiculous.

Nobody was that old. Besides, Loren didn't have the markings...that she could see. Come to think of it, she'd not seen Loren in a short-sleeved shirt, much less without one. Her curiosity piqued, Lily found she couldn't turn her brain away from her mysterious employer. There was one certain way to find out if he had the tattoos, but she wasn't willing to sacrifice her dignity to find out. Granted, he was attractive enough that she might give up a little heavy petting...but no matter how she tried to imagine herself in his arms, the face atop the body always morphed into Rowan.

Plus, the thought of Loren's hands on her felt wrong.

And she was imagining things. It dawned on her that she'd put so much stock into that stupid website that she was using it as a basis for comparison between her former lover and her current employer.

Lily set her teeth hard against the growl rising in her throat and went back to scribbling notes on her list.

She threw her pen down and breathed a sigh of disgust. He'd just offered her a full-time spot on his payroll despite the constant physical objectification. Of course, Rowan had done the same thing right before bedding her, so she couldn't split hairs there. Well, not technically. The difference was that from the first moment she'd laid eyes on Rowan, she'd wanted to climb him like a tree, or play doctor, or anything that would involve one or both of them naked and in compromising positions. And for that, she'd had her safe little world ripped open, and despite the fact that she'd been the one to do the leaving—or rather, not calling—it still frustrated her to no end that she couldn't get him out of her head.

A week into her new job, Lily's attention was pulled away by Loren's excited hand at her wrist. "I found something you need to see," he said, and tugged her to the far corner of the room. Standing amid a band of staves was a sheathed sword. The weapon stood taller than she, its hilt beginning even with her nose and ending nearly a foot above the top of her head.

"A claymore?" she asked as he pulled it from its place. He leaned it into her hands, where she was surprised by considerable weight. When it shifted, she nearly dropped it. "The work is beautiful, but I've never seen anything like it. What's the origin?"

Loren smiled and lifted the weapon easily. With one hand he lifted it and removed the sheath. The blade glistened. It looked brand new, save the stain at its tip. The metal appeared to have been dyed black.

"You are looking at a weapon of the gods," Loren said, his voice quietly reverent. "Gram, the Dragon-Slayer."

Gram. She'd heard that name before, but she couldn't remember where.

"Dragon Slayer?" she asked. She tried not to sound disbelieving, but it didn't work so well. "Where does it come from?"

"This sword was forged on Regin's anvil a hundred lifetimes ago. The old world saw it in the hands of Sigurd, Asgard's most beloved hero."

"It's Norse?" she asked. Loren nodded. Rowan. This was his area. Odd, she thought, how after years of loneliness, the two men she had found herself in close contact with had the same fascination. Inwardly shrugging, Lily wrote it off as a funny coincidence. After all, loads of people enjoyed mythology. "And you're telling me this sword was used to slay a real dragon?" Loren smirked at her, his dark stare twinkling with mischief.

"It is Norse…but even I have a hard time believing it's the real thing. My grandfather owned it for years. He swore it was real, but I'm willing to bet it's a replica."

"So you're saying the sword was real at one time, and someone made a copy of it?"

"Well," he hedged, trying to wipe the smile from his face, "I'd like to think it could have been. I'd like to believe this could be the sword that Loki himself fought to take from the humans."

Lily laughed. She couldn't help it. "Are all millionaires as kooky as you? Or is this special just for me?" Loren rewarded her with a grin, and sheathed the blade again.

"I do try to entertain," he replied with a flourish, and leaned the sword back into the corner.

"You're really fascinated by the gods, aren't you?" she asked, as she moved back toward her work station.

"I've studied them for years," he said. "The big rumor in my family is that we're descendents of a god."

"Really?" she asked, her interest piqued. "Which one?"

"Eshu…the African trickster." He moved toward her. "My grandfather said that's why our last name is what it is…in homage to him."

"Now that is interesting. And it certainly explains your penchant for playing pranks on me."

Loren chuckled and leaned on the table. "That's my way of showing you how fond I am of you. That, and the offer. Have you considered it?"

"I have…"

"And?"

"And I still don't know. Is it all right if we wait until this showing is over before I make that decision?"

"It is…" he trailed off, his gaze still fixed on hers in a way that made her feel like he could see straight into her soul. "And now that you've humored me, perhaps I can be of assistance as you move through this mess. I know what most of it is. I just can't tell you exactly where everything is."

Lily liked the sound of that. "I'd love your assistance, especially if it makes my job easier."

"Then let it be done," Loren announced. "I will unpack while you write, and we'll figure it out together. After all, with nothing but time on my hands I only have two options. I can either help or harass… and perhaps if I can get on your good side by helping, you'll agree to have dinner with me."

She fought the urge to grind her teeth. He was persistent, she had to give him that much. "I'll share a meal with you, Loren, but not in any sort of romantic way."

He smiled as he popped open a box. "Well, I must say, I feel like I've made progress already."

CHAPTER NINE

"Look at this." Dane dropped a newspaper on the table, covering Rowan's book. He grunted as he shuffled the paper away from his book. "I'm serious, Rowan. You need to read that."

"What is it?"

"Big news."

Rowan rolled his eyes and picked up the discarded paper, then folded the pages back in their proper order. He glanced down at the headline:

ANTIQUE WEAPONRY EXHIBITION
COURTESY OF THE COLLINS-GOODWIN GALLERY

Beneath the headline was a photo. Two people stood side-by-side, holding a claymore and smiling. One of them was Lily, and the sight of her beautiful face made his heart simultaneously race and seize. Then jealousy filled him as he realized the other person in the photo was a man. And seeing that man, his blood ran cold.

"Shall I begin packing?" Dane asked. Rowan stared at the black and white newsprint article a moment longer, then shook his head.

"No."

"He will try to kill you."

"I don't care," Rowan replied. Looking at the woman he loved standing beside that monster fueled his instincts, but not the instinct to run. "I have spent my whole life running from him. Whether I win or lose, this needs to end." Dane stood by, silent, as Rowan rose and stalked around the table. "He has her. He has to know where I am. Otherwise, he would not have settled here under yet another false name."

Rowan paced the length of the room, turned, and stalked back. He did this four times, all the while grumbling incoherently and muttering under his breath. He would have no peace until this was settled, one way or another. He just hated that Lily had to become involved. Rowan never stayed anywhere long, and it appeared that his pattern of duck-and-run was becoming even more of a game for Loki.

"Get out."

Rowan paused his pacing and looked at Dane. "What?"

"You heard me," his assistant said. "Get out. Go away. Find Lily if you must, but please get out of this house and stop pacing before you walk your way through the floor."

Rowan scowled. "Where the hell would I go, Dane?"

"You own three houses, a yacht, a restaurant, and a nightclub. Any one of those would be sufficient. Just go somewhere and interact with people before you lose your mind."

"It may be too late for that." Rowan really hated it when his assistant played voice of reason between the two of them. "But if you insist on making me leave, may I at least get dressed first?"

"You have fifteen minutes." Dane turned on his heels and stalked out of the room. Rowan stood in place for a long time, staring out the window at the cars moving around the square. He thought of his options — the places he could go — and none of them sounded particularly appealing. He didn't want to eat. The yacht was an impulse buy that he'd never used beyond party rental. He had never been on it for pleasure himself. The other houses were too far away, and the nightclub — another impulse buy — was even less appealing. He wasn't in the mood to dance.

But it was dark and would be a nice place to hide out.

In the thirteen days it took Lily to properly catalog Loren's collection, she had done it while ducking constant pranks, flirts, and unnerving stares. She opened every box, pulled every item out of every case, she made lists, and made notes, and had the museum send over a dozen interns to create description tags from her notes to attach to the items. She shipped most of the restoration pieces out for cleaning, but she kept some of the smaller, fragile, and more interesting pieces for her own work. The weaponry, while fascinating, disturbed her. There was so much of it, and it spanned so many different time periods, that she lost track of where the collection actually began and ended.

She even found herself fascinated by that sword...fascinated to the point where she went to the bookstore and bought several books on Nordic legends. Lily read every single story about Sigurd and Regin, and even the dragon, Fafnir. On the rare occasions that Loren would leave her alone, she crept to the corner and weighed the weapon in her hands. Part of her wanted to believe in the magic of it, to know that the black stain at the end of the blade was dragon's blood...that a true hero lived and touched the very thing in her hands. Still, the logical, rational part of her brain told her she was nuts. Told her there was no way those stories really could have happened. There were no such things as dragons, for one. Shape-shifters, she understood all too well...but dragons? No. That was going way too far.

The stories were all written as fantasy for a reason, and she knew that while Sigurd may have lived, he hadn't slain a real dragon, just as she knew that Heracles was only a murdering madman in hero's clothing.

Loren's advances still came, and she continued to ignore him. It didn't help that every time she thought she was nearing completion on the cataloging process, she found one more box tucked into one more drawer with one more bizarre artifact. Lily started to wonder if he wasn't planting them overnight in order to keep her there.

Not that it mattered. She still had to oversee the gallery while it was open. Plus, she hadn't given him an answer on his job offer. The money was good and the job easy enough, but that list of "perks" he had yet to bring her still frightened her. And like it or not, she was stuck with him for at least another two months.

Maybe…

Maybe it wouldn't be so bad. His active pursuit of her was flattering, and he was an attractive man by any number of standards. Plus he was wealthy and intelligent and provided great conversation when it wasn't about her ass or other assets. No, he wasn't Rowan, but in reality she couldn't hold that against him. It wasn't Loren's fault she'd let herself grow inexplicably attached to a monster. If anything, she should be ready to throttle Rowan for being so damned charming.

Luckily, Loren was there to break up that train of thought with a loud and surprisingly clumsy entrance.

"Hi, gorgeous," he said after a smooth recovery from a near-catastrophic collision with a gallery case. Lily, in a swift and solemn vow to adjust her outlook on life and men in general, hit him with a bright smile.

"Hi yourself," she chirped, and he paused to consider her. A sly grin curled the corners of his lips, giving him a wicked, almost sinful appearance.

"My, we're chipper this morning, aren't we?"

"We are." Feeling silly, Lily popped the lid on her newest find—a box of books—and slipped on a pair of gloves. "Uncovering the treasures of the eccentric millionaire's basement does wonders for disposition," she said. Loren laughed and settled the bag he carried on the table next to her notebook.

"Good to know my eccentricity entertains you. Danish?" He tore the bag down the side, spilling warm pastries onto her work space. She smiled, settling the stack of books to the side, and her stomach rumbled as the scent of fresh baked dough hit her nose. Her cheeks warming, she snapped off a glove and pulled a cheese Danish from the pile.

"Thank you," she said. As she lifted the pastry to her lips, she felt like a bug under Loren's microscope. He watched her intently as she took a bite and began to chew. "This is good," she offered around the food.

"I know."

"Where'd you get them?"

His grin turned impish. "From my kitchen."

She nearly choked in her surprise. "You made them?" She hadn't expected that and the astonishment showed as she paused to look back at him. A second rush of embarrassment coursed through her, no doubt staining her face with a blush.

"I did."

"Seriously?"

"Of course. Did you not expect a man like me to have culinary skill?" Now she knew she was blushing. She felt ridiculous. "After all, I am the eccentric billionaire with nothing but time on his hands." Lily ducked down behind the table again and went back to examining the books — anything to get away from his gaze.

"No, it isn't that."

"Then what?" He leaned over the table, resting his arms on the edge and smiled at her. His face was much more predatory than...no, she was not going to think about it. She promised herself she was not going to do it anymore.

"It's just…"

"You are still hung up on someone else." Lily nearly choked on the pastry clamped between her teeth. "Yes, you are that easy to read, Lily."

She took a deep breath and closed her eyes to steady her thoughts and her skittering heart. "Not anymore," she said finally. "Not really."

"Well," Loren said, his smile turning sly, "let me be the first to extend a formal invitation to dinner." Lily pushed the last bit of Danish into her mouth and chewed slowly, using the time to consider her options. She blew it with Rowan and this job was only a temporary one, so why not have some fun? She started to accept then remembered that the offer of a permanent position still hung in the balance. Lily began to question her morals…not that they mattered much anymore after her romp with Rowan. She could easily have fun with Loren…if only the whole situation didn't feel so damned *wrong*…

"I'd love to," she answered, surprising herself. Loren's eyes sparkled with new intensity, and no small amount of surprise.

"Tonight, then," he said, and motioned to the pile of Danishes. "Those are yours. I will let you work in peace." Loren turned and walked away without another word, closing the door behind him.

"That was weird," Lily muttered as she folded back the flaps on the box and slipped on a fresh glove. But she wasn't going to think about it. She had work to do.

The tomes were old and dusty, but most were in excellent condition despite the substandard storage. She wrinkled her nose against the cloud of dust that billowed up from beneath the top layer and slowly spread them across the part of the table not consumed by pastry. Most of the books were cloth-bound, some hand-written, and included a spectacular array of subjects.

She found two medical manuals, a hand-lettered bible she was willing to bet money was an authentic Wycliffe manuscript—the one book alone that could make her career if it was real—a series of journals written in what looked like German, and various propaganda pamphlets. She lost hours poring over the volumes, carefully noting dates and authors and subjects, making certain she missed nothing when it came to the details.

But as she neared the bottom of the box, one book in particular caught and held her attention. It was bound in white leather—yellowed with age—with intricate knotwork burned into its surface. She opened the cover, the spine crackling in a way that made her stomach lurch, and found only a single word on the title page.

LUPUS

The blood in her veins ran cold. A book about wolves—particularly one this old and well-decorated—usually meant some forgotten history or mythology. But this book...Lily knew its contents would take her down a road she had been afraid to walk for weeks now.

"Lily?" Loren's voice echoed through the nearly empty room, startling her into dropping the book. It landed on its spine with a crushing thump, and she winced as she squatted to retrieve it. Lily shoved the book down into her bag and picked up one of the others as his footsteps neared. Forcing calm into her breath and body, she focused on the book in her hands—some boring history about the creation of Earth. "There you are!" He leaned on the counter above her and she tried to smile at him. The action felt forced, and she knew it looked just as fake.

"Right where you left me," she replied.

"You ready for dinner?"

Ugh…dinner…she'd completely forgotten. But she had also agreed to go. With a sigh, she stood up and brushed her hands together, expelling another cloud of dust. "Just let me clean myself up a bit."

"Take your time," he said, eyes fixed on her rear as she strode across the room. Lily cringed, and had to physically bite her tongue to keep from throwing some trite insult at him.

If she'd known he planned to take her clubbing after dinner, Lily never would have agreed to the date—because a simple dinner had turned into just that. Despite her protests that she hated large groups and didn't dance, Loren insisted on slipping the doorman a ridiculous roll of bills in exchange for entrance to the club. She felt compelled to apologize to the people already in line for the intrusion, but the sharp look she received from Loren made her close her mouth without a word.

He dragged her onto the dance floor where he proceeded to feel her up while she stomped all over his toes. It started out unintentional and he didn't seem to notice, or even mind that the closer he pulled her the more damage she did. Even though she'd managed to find a decent rhythm in the song she still continued to crunch his toes beneath her heels, all the while apologizing and reminding him that she tried to warn him. But as the song ended and he kissed her, his mouth soft and warm and insistent, she forgot that she needed to apologize.

Loren's tongue swirled around hers and their bodies picked up the rhythm of the new song. With each heavy bass-beat, his hips surged against hers and his tongue swept across the line of her teeth, turning her body to a puddle of warm, tingling goo in his arms. Somewhere in the recesses of her mind, she could hear her rationality screaming to stop, that this was wrong, that he was beginning a pattern of taking advantage of her, but his hands felt so good, his kiss so smooth, that she didn't want to stop.

Lily didn't realize she was being steered away from the dance floor until her back hit the wall and Loren's roaming hands squeezed the globes of her ass. Despite his wiry frame, he was much stronger than she thought. His mouth covered hers, sucking the breath from her as he suckled at her tongue. His whole body pressed against hers, and when she felt the hard ridge of his arousal press into her belly, warning bells went off. She pushed him back enough to break contact between their mouths.

"Loren, wait…" she gasped, but the catlike smile on his face told her he wasn't finished.

"Too soon?" he asked.

"Too fast," she replied, still breathless, even as he leaned forward and brushed his lips across hers again.

"I can make you forget all about him," Loren whispered, and devoured her again.

As quickly as this new assault began, it came to an end when Loren abruptly flew backwards, sliding away from her across the floor. His retreat happened in slow motion. When he skidded to a stop, the sounds of the club crashed down on her in full focus, threatening to deafen her with the heavy bass-beats. Lily thought her mind had overloaded and played a nasty trick on her when Rowan's face materialized in front of her, his massive frame blocking her view of both Loren and the still dance floor.

"Rowan?" she said, struck dumb by his presence. "What are you doing here?"

"Protecting you," he snarled, his teeth bared in a frightening half-grimace.

"From what?"

"A mistake."

Loren's laughter cut through the noise of the club like a knife, piercing her skin with its icy tone as he stalked into view. "The great white knight has come to rescue the damsel in distress, I see," he said. His eyes were dark and cold, and while Lily could only see Rowan in quarter-profile when he turned his head, she was certain his expression was much the same.

"What the hell are you doing here?" Rowan growled.

"I was sharing an evening with my date, not that it's any of your business." Loren causally brushed off the sleeves of his shirt and tucked the hem back into his pants, repairing the damage Rowan had done. Tension popped between them like arcs of electricity. Lily could feel it crawling over her skin, threatening to drown her in frustration and fear.

"Why come here?"

"Public place."

"Bastard."

"Rowan!" Lily snapped, stepping between them. The sight of him — the strong, possessive, alpha-male — sent a shock of awareness bolting through her. His handsome face, even contorted with anger, tangled her heart up in knots. "What the hell is going on?"

"Your friend," Loren said, stepping up to sling an arm around her shoulders, "doesn't seem to like me very much."

Lily twisted out of his grip to glare up at him. "What did you do to him to make him not like you?" she shouted over the music.

"I don't know what you mean," Loren shouted back, but the hard set of his jaw told her he was lying. She didn't have to hear his voice to know that.

"Get out of here," Rowan said over the top of her head. His breath ruffled the small hairs across the back of her neck. She suppressed a shiver, and rounded on him. His vision was still trained hard on Loren.

"And who are you to decide that?" she asked. Again, the sight of him was like a punch in the chest, and she had to focus just to keep breathing.

"The owner," Rowan and Loren said at the same time. She fell short on a response, gawking back and forth between them. Even in the relative dimness of the club she saw Rowan's face pale. "And he should have known not to come in here," Rowan added.

Lily's mind reeled. They knew each other. And they hated each other. And Rowan owned the damned club. This must be the trouble Rowan talked about.

"All right, outside...both of you," she shouted, and started for the front door. Rowan caught her wrist and pulled her around behind a curtain, into a dark hallway. The touch of his fingers on her skin burned; threatened to derail her completely, despite the fact that she'd only moments before been kissing another man. And enjoying it. Then the cold night air rushed over her and his touch left her. Lily turned to face the pair of them, taking a deep, hard breath to steady her jangled nerves. "Now, will one of you please explain to me what the hell is going on?"

Loren and Rowan caught each other's stare, holding in that pattern for a long moment. Neither spoke.

"Rowan...how do you know him?"

"We go way back," he said through clenched teeth. She was afraid of what that meant. "Your boyfriend," he spat the word at her, "has a bad habit of stealing things from me."

"First of all, Loren isn't my boyfriend."

"Didn't look that way inside."

"I work for him, you idiot. As for that kiss...I hardly had time to process it before you threw him halfway across the room!"

"My prerogative as owner," Rowan replied, unrepentant.

"Go to hell, Keir," Loren snapped, obviously having had enough of this game.

"Fuck you," Rowan said. "Fucking poacher."

"If you wanted her, you should have marked her."

"I am not a barbarian."

"What?" Lily interjected, but went unnoticed.

"So the chest-beating He-Man bullshit is considered civilized in your world?" Loren asked with a smirk.

"You will destroy her."

"And it is no concern of yours."

"It is."

Loren rolled his eyes and laughed, a deep, sardonic chuckle that rattled Lily's nerves. She had no idea what this argument was really about, but at the center of it was not where she wanted to be. "Don't give me some lame line about her being your mate."

"Hurt her and I will tear you limb from limb," Rowan threatened.

"I'd like to see you try."

"There won't be any trying, kitten." The air shimmered around Rowan's form. His eyes, normally that soft sea-and-sky color Lily loved, had dilated, shifting to black. His teeth looked sharper, his fingernails more like claws.

"BOTH OF YOU SHUT UP!" Lily screamed, and both men froze. She swallowed around the frustrated lump in her throat. She knew how close Rowan was to losing it, knew that Loren had provoked him. No matter how she spun it in her head, Rowan was the monster she wished he wasn't, and while the offered protection flattered her, it also frightened her.

There was something deeper happening here, she knew. She had no idea what they were really arguing about, but she knew without a doubt that she was at the crux of the fight, and was ultimately the catalyst for whatever would happen from here on out.

"Now will one of you idiots please put aside the

testosterone and *calmly* explain to me what is going on? Loren?"

"Keir here is jealous because he let you get away."

"No," Rowan countered, his voice taking on an edge of desperation that set her nerves on high-alert. Even with what little she knew of him, she knew he was reasonable. And he did not sound reasonable right now. "He is dangerous, Lily."

"I knew this was a mistake," she muttered, pinching the bridge of her nose. This had to end or someone was going to get hurt. "Look," she started, forcing calm into her voice, "I don't know where this misguided sense of duty has come from, but as flattering as it is on both sides, it's a little creepy."

"He's jealous," Loren said at the same moment Rowan muttered, "He is dangerous." Throwing her hands up in disgust, Lily turned and stalked away, hailing a cab despite both their protests, and gave the driver Loren's address so she could pick up her car.

Furious, Rowan turned as soon as Lily was out of sight and backed Loren against the wall of the building. His chest ached, his head throbbed, and he wanted nothing more than to drag her back, push her up against the wall, and take her in a way that left no doubt who she belonged to. But Loren had seen to it that such things wouldn't happen.

Rowan growled, and the smaller man shrank against the brick. He never broke eye contact.

"Destroy me if you must, but if you do anything to hurt her…" he growled.

"I'm just cleaning up your mess, wolf."

"If you hurt her, I will tear your throat out, cat."

Loren's lip curled into a sneer. "After six hundred years of your whining, I have a very hard time believing you will do more than fight. Besides, I might enjoy the challenge." He brushed past Rowan and stalked toward his car. Rowan remained rooted to the spot, staring at the blank wall with a head full of violence.

CHAPTER TEN

Lily flung herself onto the couch and pulled a throw-pillow down over her head. Why are men so damn impossible? she thought. All the way home she'd alternated between fury and tears, all the while humiliated by both reactions. The humiliation only seemed to fuel the tears, which in turn led to the anger.

She growled and punched at the couch, bruising her knuckles on the wood frame beneath the fabric. Pain licked through her fingers, and she fought the urge to scream in melodramatic agony, frustration, or any other emotion that surfaced from her battered hand.

"Damn," she whimpered, turning the word into a whine as she sat up. Tears pricked the corners of her eyes, but she stubbornly sniffed them back. This night had turned into a monumental disaster, and both men in her life were in some way responsible. Lily glanced around the room, determined to not let her gaze land on the expensive shopping bags stacked next to her fireplace. She hadn't touched them save

149

to move them from the couch, and she didn't intend to do so now. Instead, she focused on her oversized purse and its contents, spilled all over the armchair. The book she'd pilfered from Loren's collection lay amongst the clutter, all but forgotten until her eyes found its worn leather cover.

Warning bells went off in her head as she stretched over the arm of the couch and pulled the book free from the personal wreckage. It smacked of knowledge and danger, but also of irreversible truth.

Lupus.

Wolf.

Lily turned it over in her hands, testing its weight, savoring the rasp of old leather against her fingertips. A lump rose in her throat when her thumb slipped over the uneven pages. With great effort, she swallowed it back and cracked the cover.

Pages and pages of hand-written text glared up at her. Many of the words were written so hastily and in such an old manner that for several moments she scarcely understood what it all meant, but then one word came into sharp focus and she realized exactly what it was she held.

Wolfe.

That one word was clear and unmistakable, and her heart bumped hard against her ribcage in response. The image of Rowan's body trapped in the shimmering agony of the shift sprang to mind. She cringed.

> When the dragon Fafnir's descendents agreed to protect the ringe, their spirits embodied the visage of the wolfe. Sigurd did flee the cave, taking with him a scale from the Great Dragon's bodye, jewels with which to free him from the indenture of Regin by way of proof of the dragon's demise. For himself he did take onlye the ring as a gift to his love. The wolfe, the strong and courage-us warrior, did seek out Sigurd and remove from his possession the ringe.

It's all nonsense, she told herself, and tried to ignore the meaning in the words, to write them off as the ramblings of a lunatic. It was only a coincidence. It had to be. Perhaps the reason Loren owned the book was because he bought into the myth so readily.

But the more she read, the harder it became to ignore the ring of truth in them. To further the disconcerting fear, she read words she'd already committed to memory. From that stupid website.

Fulle Moone
A forced change at the fulle-moone is a common error. The pulle of the moone is to

151

a wolfe like the tide. A wolfe will always experiense the lunatic frensey, how-euer it does not always occur in the forme of a forced shifte. The driue to shifte, and to mate, becomes much too strong for anye but a true Alpha to resiste. Euen an Alpha will experiense the draw to finde his Omega.

Lily threw the book to the coffee table and raced across the room, flipping back her calendar to the date of her "interview" with Rowan. Horror-struck, she stared at the small, darkened circle in the upper left corner of that date.

"No," she whimpered and dropped the pages back into place. Lily refused to let herself believe any of this nonsense…at least, she kept telling herself it was. That she'd slept with him on the night of a full moon meant little. A coincidence. Still…

She picked up the book and continued to read.

Should an Alpha meete his Omega, the urge to mate will be much too stronge to ignore. The female will be drawne to the wolfe. Once the mating process begins, the change will often be inuoluntarie.

Lily dropped the book back to the couch and wailed in frustration. Every word of it was true.

Rowan was like a drug in her system. He changed around her. And despite the time away from him, she'd still felt the urge to crawl into his arms when he came near. She'd gone into the club with Loren, kissed him even, but...

She'd forgotten about him when Rowan showed up.

Rowan told her they went way back, too. What the hell did that mean? And why did Loren have a book on wolf shifters? Lily had had her doubts about Loren, but now she had so many questions that her head swam. Before she fully registered what she was doing, she'd picked up the phone and dialed Rowan's telephone number. He answered on the second ring.

"Tell me in ten words or less why you interfered," she snapped.

"Loren isn't what you think. He's dangerous."

"I'm sure he would say the same of you."

"I am quite honestly shocked that he didn't."

"You didn't give him the chance."

Rowan sighed into her ear, and in her mind she could see the pained look on his face. She shook her head to clear the image. She was angry with him, damn it.

"Listen to me, Lily," he said, his voice thick with some unnamed emotion. "You need to get away from him. He is a dangerous man, and now that he knows my connection to you I fear you may be in great danger."

"What is going on?"

"It's best if you don't know."

Lily huffed. "You expect me to quit my job based on some hunch that you won't even explain?"

"It isn't a hunch."

"But you still won't explain."

"I wish I could."

On the coffee table, her cell phone buzzed, signaling an incoming text message. She snapped it up and read it, debating whether she should be disgusted or amused.

"Loren is on his way over," she blurted, because she knew it would annoy Rowan. Silence greeted her, followed by the faint sound of grinding teeth.

"I'll be there first."

Lily rolled her eyes. "You really are a piece of work, you know that?" On the other end of the line, Rowan tried to interrupt, but she ignored him. "First you lure me in with the promise of a job that doesn't exist just to get me into your bed. Nice job on that one." She let loose a derisive snort. "Then you drop a bomb on me about the existence of the supernatural and your part in it...just so I'll sleep with you again. And after that you prattle on about me being your mate before disappearing. No contact. At all. Then you attack my boss, make assumptions as to my relationship with him, and tell me you're going to show up here, all in the name of chivalry..." She took a deep breath, prepared to start up again when a knock at the door startled her. "He's here," she said instead, and jerked open the door.

And dropped the phone.

"Is he really?" Rowan said, smirking down at her. He carried a smile on his lips, but his eyes were full of concern. Lily stared up at him, at his huge frame filling her doorway. Her jaw flapped like a loose hinge while she battled the urge to leap into his arms.

"What the hell?" she muttered.

"I was on my way over anyway. I had to be certain you were safe." He reached out and traced the ridge of her cheek with a gentle fingertip. The smart comment she had prepared died in her throat. Fear was etched deep into the lines of his face, coloring his features with a smoky film. "Come with me, Lily." Her mouth went dry, and while her body screamed yes, yes, yes! she remained rooted to the spot, puzzling him out.

"Where?"

"Anywhere but here."

"But Loren—"

"Will kill you." Desperation mingled with fear bolted through his features, and the matter-of-fact way he said it left little room for argument or disbelief. "Please." She didn't know what to do. Anything that could frighten Rowan that much was definitely worth worrying about, but she did run out on Loren. And she did still work for him. "Tell him you're staying with a friend."

"But I have to –"

"And if you insist on going back, I will see that you get to work in the morning," Rowan offered. "Please do this for me." He held up his hands in a frustrating and familiar gesture. "Hands off, I promise."

"If I don't show up, he'll suspect something."

"I highly doubt he's oblivious to the situation now," Rowan said flatly.

She had no doubt he'd keep that promise, whether she wanted him to or not. Groaning, she turned and swept her things back into her purse.

"Where are you taking me?"

"My guest room. Pack a few things...and hurry." The urgency in his voice propelled her into motion, but his big hand on her wrist stopped her. "Take those," he said, pointing to the untouched shopping bags. Her whole body burned with embarrassment, but she had no time to explain or to apologize as he blew past her and scooped them up. She scarcely had time to sling her purse over her shoulder and step into her shoes before he pulled her out the door.

"You going to tell me what's going on?"

"On the way. Come on." Rowan shoved her into the passenger's seat of his car and slammed the door.

It wasn't until they reached the city limits that she realized she'd left the book on her sofa.

Loren stared at the book lying on the couch. Thieving bitch. She had to be working for the wolf, otherwise she wouldn't have given it a second thought. And of course she was staying the night with a friend. He'd seen the unfamiliar car drive away. Loren swallowed and mentally dampened the rising rage.

The itch started in his feet and swept through his body like fire. For a moment, the world went black, and when he opened his eyes the color had drained from it. He sniffed, testing the air and tasting the bitter tang of wolf. He felt, rather than heard, the growl that escaped his muzzle, and snorted against the stench. She swore she was over him, but this time she really had gone too far.

Loren padded silently back through the house into the spare bedroom and leapt through the broken window. With any luck, she'd not know of his intrusion.

The power coursed through his lithe feline form as he stretched and broke into a sprint. He knew these woods well, enjoyed hunting them, and upon picking up the wolf's scent leading to her nearly a month ago, had used them to discover just how easy it was for a simple human to be persuaded. Unfortunately, that persuasion worked on both sides.

It was time to up the stakes.

Lily stared at the closed door, fuming. Rowan, ever the damned gentleman, ushered her in and quickly put walls and planks of hinged, brass-handled wood between them. Damn chivalry, she thought. Damn it to hell.

The entire car ride back to his home was silent and filled with tension. The air practically sparked between them as he opened the door and ushered her inside, holding all of her things in one hand. She still felt the need to apologize to him for not being gracious about his gifts, but she still couldn't bring herself to do it. And it didn't help that he hadn't even given her the opportunity to speak before pulling the door closed and disappearing into the depths of the building.

"I'm losing my mind," she said out loud. One moment she was ready to throttle him for hijacking her night, but as soon as she stopped to think about it she wanted to sneak into his bed and surprise him. The attraction didn't make sense. Neither did the repulsion.

She resolutely ignored her subconscious as it attempted to remind her of the book.

Turning, Lily paced the room, stubbornly glancing back and forth between the door and the bags. It had been almost a month since he purchased those things for her. She couldn't even remember what was in each of the bags. Still, her pride refused to let her pull out the bright paper and unwrap them. Lily told herself it was because she wanted a shower first, to wash away the grime of a failed evening.

Then it hit her that she didn't have anything to wear to bed. Growling, she stalked over to the bags, snatched them up, and upended them into the center of the king-size guest bed. Tissue-wrapped items fell out and bounced across the duvet, some falling open to reveal expensive shoes while others flattened as the air puffed out of them.

She recognized the two dresses, the scrap of fabric that was much too short to be called a skirt he had insisted she let him buy, the pair of black pants and…

Wait a minute.

A piece of pink tissue tumbled open to reveal something small, soft, and black. Lily didn't remember seeing him purchase anything black. Nudging the paper away, she lifted the item by its thin straps, and gasped at the sight.

A satin and lace negligee. With a matching robe lying beneath it.

"Oh, my God."

She couldn't believe he'd actually had the nerve to buy it. Assuming he'd purchased that for her to wear with him, Lily threw it back to the bed and rolled her eyes. At least she had something to sleep in now.

Not that she wanted to sleep. Seeing that pathetic excuse for a nightgown tipped her mind into a wild, rolling tumble. She was essentially a prisoner in his home with no means of escape, trapped between some rich and twisted supernatural mutant and whatever the hell Loren was. Rowan still hadn't explained what was going on. Damn it, she needed answers.

With a plan forming in her mind, Lily snatched up the scrap of fabric, pulled a towel from the rack, and disappeared into the bathroom.

Rowan paced the room like a caged animal. The walls were too close, the ceiling too low. And the woman on the other end of the house much too tempting. It was foolish to bring her here, he knew, but it was the only place she would be safe from Loki. Only, he was not entirely certain that he could keep her safe from himself. He'd promised her he'd behave himself, and the one thing keeping him away was that she still smelled of feline. The stench infuriated him...and yet he felt the need to cover her with his own scent, to obliterate any trace of the creation that was Loren Eshu.

The shower started, and he cursed under his breath. If that one thing could keep him away, it wouldn't for long. Even across the house he heard the spray change as she stepped into it. All at once he remembered the sight of her, naked and wanton, writhing beneath him.

Growling, he flung open the balcony doors and stepped out into the cool night air. The breeze did little to alleviate the fire licking through his veins. He should leave—set the alarms to protect her and escape into the city. He shouldn't stay. It would be no good for either of them. But even for all his strength, he was too weak to stay away from her. Gods help him, he wanted her in the most irrational way.

The water shut off on the other side of the building and his face bunched in a grimace. Rowan's hands itched to hold her again. The pain already coursed through his limbs. He needed her, and he knew that another coupling would mean his end.

"Rowan?"

Fuck.

He'd been so lost in his head that he'd not heard the door open or her footsteps until it was too late. The sweet smell of her skin hit him and he crumbled inside, his self-control shattering into a thousand tiny pieces. He turned and his mouth fell open as he looked at her. The small gown draped over her curves as deliciously as he'd imagined, stopping at the tops of her thighs. Black fabric clung to pale, milk-white skin and a small, nervous smile turned her cheeks up.

"Lily," he croaked, and cleared his throat to clear the rust from his voice. "You should be in bed." Sweet Hell, he was going to lose it if she didn't leave.

"Not sleepy."

"So you thought coming over here…" he trailed off. She wrung her hands together in nervous fashion, her eyes darting back and forth around the room, but never looking at him.

"I…I don't know," she said, already moving across the floor to perch on the edge of the bed. Rowan closed his eyes to keep them from rolling back in his head. The woman was more temptation than she knew. "I don't know what's going on. I'm afraid and I don't want to be alone right now. There's too much going on in my head."

"Yours?" Rowan laughed and shook his head. "Try having two separate consciousnesses in your head all the time."

Lily stared at Rowan as he came toward her, unable to make sense of what he'd said. "Two?"

162

"Always." His handsome face twisted into a mask of something that resembled pain. She wanted to reach for him, to smooth away the ache that had him so tangled up, but the moment she said his name and his attention focused on her, her nerve vanished. She knew before she ever donned this silly costume that she could never be the brazen temptress, and why she had even bothered to try was beyond her. "I always carry two sets of thoughts, and they rarely match."

"Wow."

"Times like this are rare...when the two are one."

"Must be a powerful thought." She dared a glance up at him, and met a burning gaze.

"It is," he whispered. Lily's throat went dry. She attempted to swallow.

"What's the thought?" She immediately wanted to regret asking, but couldn't. His gaze turned to a glower. From his pacing near the window, he was suddenly across the room, looming over her in the space of half a breath. His mouth hovered inches above hers.

"To strip you naked and fuck you until you scream my name," he whispered. "Promise be damned." His mouth closed over hers, sending sparks of fire tumbling through her body. She could not think, could scarcely do anything but feel as his tongue swept across hers and one big hand cradled the back of her head. He tasted of whiskey and spice, and his familiar scent overpowered her senses, even when her back landed against the bed and his weight settled over her. His kiss was fierce, desperate. Hungry. He needed her as much as she needed him.

Rowan's hands were everywhere, rasping across the soft fabric of her gown, pushing it up over her belly to reveal the small scrap of matching fabric covering her sex. He sank to his knees, gazing reverently at her overheated body before pressing his lips to the sensitive skin just above her navel, then chased his hand up her body to the valley between her breasts. Each touch of his mouth to her body added to the blaze building between her legs. Lily moaned, her breath escaping in a rush. She clasped at his head, letting the soft silk of his blond hair slide through her fingers as he licked and kissed his way back to her lips.

"Rowan..." she breathed before he claimed her mouth again. She wanted to speak but couldn't form coherent thoughts as she lay there feeling his lips, his hands...him.

The world shifted. His mouth never left hers, even with the confused rush of air that found her straddling his hips, his hands kneading the globes of her ass. Lily gasped, knowing she should stop this even as she licked a path along his jaw and down his neck. She ground her sex against him, feeling the hard ridge of his arousal press back. With each sweep of her body, he let out a strangled groan that reverberated through her body and settled deep in her womb. Rowan shifted his hips against her, pressing harder against her center, mimicking the movements she knew he would use to drive her to mindlessness. Each movement created delicious friction, pushed her closer to frenzy. Impatient, Lily reached between them, finding the waistband of his shorts, and tugged it down. Her knuckles brushed the slick skin of his cock, and Rowan shivered, hands tightening on her waist even as he raised his hips to help push the offending clothing away.

Closing her fingers around his length, Lily stroked once, twice, swirling her thumb around the swollen head before he pushed her hand away and surged up, brushing the lips of her throbbing sex. In the same breath she levered her body down, taking the full length of him inside in one movement, the thin string of her underwear snapping under the pressure and popping back against her clit.

A cry echoed through the room, and Lily realized as he lifted her body and pulled her back down that it had come from her. Rowan caught the hem of her gown and jerked it over her head, then latched onto one full, aching nipple and suckled hard. Lily squealed, bucking against the combined sensations of his mouth on her breast and his cock moving deep inside her, lost in the taste, feel, and smell of him.

Her body moved of its own accord, desperately seeking release. Lily rose and fell, the wet slap of skin echoing in between her cries of pleasure. He filled her so completely, stretched her wide, and thrust hard, each movement driving her closer and closer to breaking. His hands shook as he clutched at her body, dragging and pulling her where he wanted her. She felt like a rag doll, tossed around for his own pleasure.

One hand moved between them, his calloused thumb brushing the small bundle of nerves he found there, and sent her rocketing over the edge. Lily's mouth opened in a breathless scream as her body clenched around him, his big hands easily keeping her body moving, increasing the sensations. The edges of her vision sparkled, threatening to fade to black as ripples of pleasure coursed through her, radiating from her spasming sex, through her fingers and toes. Rowan's mouth found hers, his hands closed tightly on her waist, and he surged up hard against her with a groan. Warmth spread through her as he forced himself deep inside her, pulsing and shivering in orgasm.

All at once, he threw her backwards and leapt from the bed, the frightening, familiar wolf bursting into view and landing in a howling heap on the balcony across the room. Lily smothered a startled cry behind her hands. She stared at the beast, shaken to her core by the sight. The beast's shoulders rose and fell with labored breaths, a low whine rattling in its throat. She laid one trembling hand over her stuttering heart, and after a moment slipped to the edge of the bed.

Rowan's intelligent blue eyes stared back at her, the set of his face apologetic.

Sliding from mind-blowing sex to the worst fear of her life took no more than a moment, but as she faced the monster on the other side of the room, her heart pounded for an entirely different reason. If she intended to have any sort of relationship with this... this man, then she had to face this.

Slowly, Lily crossed the room toward him, stopping several paces away to watch him. She reached for him, squeaking in surprise when he bumped his head against her palm. The feel of his soft, smooth fur rustling across her fingers thrilled her. A small, tentative smile crossed her lips.

"I must be crazy," she said. The barking noise Rowan made sounded suspiciously like a laugh. She cut her eyes at him. "Hush," Lily commanded, and a startled giggle burst out of her throat. "It's like having a pet!" she cried, and received an unamused look as she giggled and stroked the top of his head. The big wolf snorted and paced around her, leaning against her belly. She knelt to look him in the face, but as she reached out to stroke the fur along his shoulder, his demeanor changed. The beast's long snout curled back into a snarl and he turned to face the open balcony doors, leaning against her and pushing her back toward the center of the room. "Rowan...what is it?" she asked, panic rising to choke away her earlier euphoria as the fur along his spine stood on end. He howled.

The concern in her voice scarcely registered. She couldn't know what he'd sensed, what terrible odor lurked just beyond the walled garden.

Fucking cat.

The poor girl was confused, yes, but it was for her own good. If she really knew what had come to pass since their meeting… If she knew what sort of trouble he'd led her into…

Rowan organized his thoughts against the rush of feral aggression and reached out through his mind to pull his human nature back to the surface. Itching, followed by needles of pain, coursed through his body, and as the fur receded, a thin sheen of sweat broke out across his skin. Bones, twisting and contorting with the change, echoed sickening pops as the joints reformed into a human body.

Rising to his feet, Rowan surged forward, slamming the balcony doors closed. He flipped the multiple locks, drew the curtains, and leaned against them. He drew in several deep breaths, searching for calm.

"Rowan, what is going on?" Her voice sounded desperate, panicked. "Tell me everything right now or I'm leaving."

"You can't leave," he replied. Rowan turned to face her, stung by the tears that coursed down her cheeks. "It's too dangerous."

"Well, don't you think I should know what the danger is so I can avoid it?" She was nothing if not logical, even when upset. He cringed and moved past her to sit on the edge of the bed.

"Remember when I told you there was trouble associated with me?" he asked. She whimpered, seeming to notice her nakedness, and crossed her arms over her chest as she nodded. "Well, this is it."

"What is it?" she prodded, padding back across the room to draw the bedspread up around her body.

"Loren."

"So you've said," she snorted, wiping her face with the backs of her hands as she slipped into the bed. He wanted her closer, but she stayed as far away as she could get while still keeping her body covered. "But what specifically?"

"What do you know of him?"

"Well," she perched on the mattress and drew her knees up to her chest, "he's also in his mid-thirties," she shot a sharp look at him as she said it, "and he's an eccentric millionaire art collector that supposedly inherited his fortune and collection from wealthy grandparents." Rowan couldn't stop the horrified laugh that tore loose from his throat.

"And you believe that?"

"You just asked what I knew." She scowled, and the look froze his laughter. "You also said you two have a past. Is he some sort of shifter too?"

Gods, this woman knew how to get right to the point. Any other time he would appreciate that quality, but this was conversation he had been dreading since he first lost control of his form and discovered that she was The One.

"He is. However he is not like me...not at all."

"You called him 'kitten.' I'm assuming he shifts into a cat?"

"Panther."

CHAPTER ELEVEN

"Panther."

Lily's blood ran cold. "The sightings…"

"Were of Loren," Rowan confirmed. "When the first sighting was reported, I ran the woods and found his scent."

She swallowed. "Where?"

"Concentrated around your home. He likely picked up my scent around you. I can assure you it was the catalyst for his hiring you—you were a way for him to keep track of me. Your skills turned out to be an unexpected asset for him." Rowan reached across the vast expanse of bed to take her by the shoulders and turn her to face him. "Never, never underestimate him, Lily. He is a trickster. He will kill you if he sees the need arise."

"That's good to know," she snorted. Once again in the space of seconds, Rowan left her mind reeling. Lily still had no idea exactly what the conflict was. As far as this new information about Loren having a second nature as well, she could not process it, however true it rang from his lips. And why was it always that the people in her life complicated things so? "Why me?" she asked after a long moment. Rowan's big hand brushed gently over her cheek, and a ghost of a smile appeared on his sad, beautiful mouth.

"Because I want you," he said. "Because he knows that after six hundred years, any human woman that can bring about my change is one I will protect to the death."

Lily stared at him, dumbstruck. Emotions shifted across his face in rapid succession, never staying long enough for her to pinpoint. The only one she could hang onto for more than a few seconds was anger.

"What kind of war have you dragged me into, Rowan?" Something flashed in his eyes and he rose from the bed to pace the floor. Still thought-shatteringly naked and without the least bit of thought toward that state. Not a good sign...definitely not.

"I wish I could say your terminology was wrong," he sighed, "but what this is...is a war. I never should have brought you into this, Lily. I was a fool to think I could have you. To think I could have a life free of this struggle."

She would sort out the romantic intentions later. Right now she had to figure out this war, and do it fast. Lily reached for her discarded robe and, shrugging into it, crossed the room to where Rowan paced.

"I'm assuming you barricaded us inside because he's out there?"

"Yes."

"Where exactly?"

"I do not know... Close."

As she watched him, Lily mentally paged through the book she'd stolen from Loren. One passage stood out in her mind.

"Does this have anything to do with Fafnir?"

Rowan froze, turning to stare at her. "How do you know that name if you know nothing of the histories?"

"I'm assuming that's a 'yes'?"

"How could you know it?"

Reluctantly, Lily relayed the story of how she found and took the book, and how reading it was what pushed her to call him. Rowan listened with new resolve, his face cold and impassive as stone while she recounted the passage in the book about the dragon and his death.

"I need to see this book," he said when she stopped to breathe.

"It's at my house. I left it on the couch when you rushed me out. We could go get it."

"No, I am certain he has already been there."

Lily rolled her eyes and tightened the robe around her body. She felt cold. The weight of Rowan's admissions bore down on her shoulders, making her tired. It had been a long day, starting with Loren's odd display of domesticity, and an even longer night now.

"So how is it that an old Norse myth can have so much bearing on us today?"

"The common myth is wrong," he said, "as so many are. You have heard others say that in all mythology there is a kernel of truth, yes?" Lily nodded, watching him with an odd sense of disconnection. Almost like she was watching herself as well. "Fafnir did not steal the dwarven hoard to gloat. He stole it to protect his father."

"But the myth says the cursed ring made him kill his father."

"He did kill his father, but not for the reason you think." Rowan grabbed a pair of jeans and pulled them over his hips. "Come with me. You are part of this now, and I need to show you something."

She pulled her robe tighter around her shoulders, and had to tighten the belt twice before she was out of the room—the satin had a way of falling loose—and followed him through the building into the gallery. It seemed an odd destination, and she had a brief flashback to Loren acting much the same. It unnerved her, but as the lights came up, Rowan towed her to a case on the far end of the room. It held a single item, and the sight of it caused Lily's breath to catch in her throat.

"The ring…"

Rowan flipped the door on the case open and lifted the ring from its stand. The cool, gold band was heavier than Lily thought it would be as he placed it in her palm. It reverberated with power. She felt the gentle hum, weighed the metal while the current coursed through her fingers. "The source of this war," he said.

"I...I still don't understand." He reached into the case and pulled a small pouch from beneath the ring's stand.

"The dwarf-king, Andvari, forged this ring several lifetimes ago, but it was stolen before he could own it." Lily went numb. This conversation was too close to the one she'd had with Loren. This made it too real. And she didn't know what to believe.

"The story says it's cursed."

"The only curse upon this ring is that Loki will never hold it. Human greed is what brought about the death of Fafnir and his family. Sigurd murdered Fafnir for the ring, but not before Fafnir bore a daughter of his own in secret."

"Is there written proof of this?"

"No."

"Then why should I believe it?"

Rowan scoffed. "Do you find it so hard to believe that humans do not want to prove the existence of the old gods?"

"Proof?"

He tapped the ring in her hand. "Proof of Loki's trickery."

"Why should I believe any of this?"

"Because Fafnir's daughter was my grandmother." Lily gasped, and the ring clattered to the floor. Her hold on reality shifted, and Rowan caught her just before she collapsed into darkness.

Groaning, Rowan lifted her limp body into his arms. They were too far past safe to stop now, and though the information had overwhelmed her, she had to know the rest. He bent and picked up the ring, tucking it and the pouch into his pocket before locking the case and taking Lily back to the bedroom. This was the one part of his past he hated—the gods and monsters mystery. For the thousandth time since meeting Lily, Rowan wished his life could be that of a normal human.

He laid her across the bed and went to his dresser, where he pulled a gold chain from one of the many boxes and threaded the ring onto it. While Lily slept, he clasped it around her neck then pulled her into his arms where she lay without moving. When she woke two hours later, she woke disoriented. Her panicked gaze scanned the room, but when she finally found him above her, she relaxed back into his arms.

"Rowan," she croaked, her voice thick with sleep. He kissed her forehead and inhaled her sweet scent, enjoying her heady flavor. She hummed against his chest and stretched. He wanted her, but his selfish desires would have to wait.

"Welcome back," he said.

"Please tell me I dreamed all of that." Rowan tapped the ring lying against the hollow of her throat.

"I am afraid not, my love." He chuckled when she groaned, and pulled her closer. "There is more, too."

She covered her face with her hands and whimpered. "You mean to tell me it gets worse?" Her voice dripped with sarcasm. "Next you're going to tell me that Loren is a descendent of Loki, right?"

He hesitated, amazed again by her ability to sniff out the truth, and felt a small smile curl the corner of his mouth. "Something like that."

"Oh, God!" she wailed, and buried her face against his chest. "This is so beyond ridiculous!"

"So it would seem. As much as I would love to say it is not, this is all the truth."

Lily sighed and sat up to look at Rowan. The ring lay cold against her chest, a heavy reminder of the mess she'd gotten herself into. She couldn't bring herself to question its placement yet, but even so, something did not add up.

"Loren's last name is Eshu. He said something once about being related to the god."

"What do you know about Eshu?" Rowan asked. Lily thought back to her classes and reference books, and the few things Loren told her. Turned out it wasn't much.

"He's a trickster." She searched Rowan's face for information, but found nothing but calm patience. "He could look like two different things to people standing side-by-side."

"He is not one of the old gods."

Lily waited for Rowan to continue, but he remained silent. "I don't follow."

"After the death of Hreidmar, Freyja beat Loki with her bare hands, then demanded that Odin banish him from Asgard. Since Loki was responsible for the Gods' capture, which ultimately led to the theft of the ring—"

"Odin didn't banish him?"

"Not exactly. He demanded that he be chained and have the poison of the scorpion dripped on his body for eternity."

"But how did he—"

"End up in Africa?" Lily nodded. "Anansi."

"The spider-god?"

"Also a trickster. Loki loved to play games at the expense of others. Anansi was alone and lonely, and for centuries, Loki's ruses were blamed on the spider. One night the two came face to face, the Great Spider and the Panther. The villagers saw the confrontation, and from it the god Eshu was born."

Lily lay back against the pillows and scrubbed her palms over her face. The whole of European mythology was being rewritten as they spoke, and while it was a fantastic story, she still couldn't quite wrap her head around it. "That doesn't work," she said after several long minutes of contemplation. "Loki was chained. He couldn't be in Africa."

"True," Rowan agreed. "But the trickster had many ruses, many faces, and many charms. It was not long before Loki broke the bonds and led the giants to Ragnarok."

"Ragnarok?"

"The apocalypse…so to speak. But his attempts at destroying Asgard failed, and Loki knew he was never to return. The exile alone is more than enough to appease the other gods and keep the All-Father's hands clean."

"So…back up. How is Loren related to Eshu?" she asked. He fixed her with a hard stare. She was trying to catch up, to understand, but the overwhelming information dump still had her head spinning. "He's Loki's grandson?" Rowan shook his head, the barest hint of a smile haunting his mouth. "Son?" The smile widened, yet he shook his head again. She started to respond again, but the thought was just too absurd. The look on Rowan's face told her he knew what she wanted to say, yet she still couldn't. If she were right… "No," she blurted and her eyes widened.

"He has lived many lifetimes with many names and many faces. He has been a charmer, a drifter, and a criminal…but always a god."

"No."

Rowan nodded toward her neck. "It all goes back to greed. Loki wants the treasure. He thought he would be able to take it back once Hreidmar's family caved in on itself. Only, he did not know of Fafnir's woman, or of the child."

"Wouldn't Odin have told him? I mean, they were brothers, right?"

"The All-Father never divulged all of his secrets. Of course he knew of our existence, but to turn again on the people he had endangered… Mischievous, he might have been. Cruel, never."

"So why you?" She drew her knees up to her chin and rested her cheek on them. "And why a wolf?"

"Fafnir's decision to take the form of a dragon seemed a flawless plan. With one exception."

"Sigurd knew the secret to bring him down."

"Yes." Rowan opened the pouch he'd brought with them and dumped its contents into Lily's hand. A single, shimmering dragon scale. She blinked at it several times, unable to comprehend the iridescent, near-invisible thing as the light around her flickered on its surface. "One unguarded place over the heart, and the chosen trophy of Sigurd."

"This is unreal."

"My grandmother, after Fafnir's death, was tasked with finding and guarding the hoard. The wolf is a tracker. Loyal, noble blood demands a noble form. And a creature as fantastic as a dragon sadly does not fit well into human history."

"So I've noticed. But what's Loki's part in this?"

"Because the ring was used as part of the payment for the death of Fafnir's brother Otr, Loki, like Andvari, never truly got to own it. It was he who convinced Regin to create the sword that would take the life of his brother. Loki sees the ring as payment for his exile."

Lily rolled her eyes. She was exhausted. "I can't think about this anymore." Rowan pulled her into his chest and held her close.

"Then we will sleep. I would feel better if you agreed not to leave me in the morning." He yawned loudly.

"I have to work tomorrow."

"Leaving is dangerous."

"If I don't show up, he'll be suspicious, Rowan."

Rowan stilled as if thinking this through. After a moment, he nodded. "Perhaps a trip behind enemy lines would be good for us…even if I do not like it."

Lily groaned. "I'm not dealing with this tonight. I have to be at work by eight. Wake me up at seven." She crawled under the covers and pulled them up over her head, then fought the urge to smack Rowan as he slid behind her, chuckling.

"One more question," Lily said after a moment.

"Yes?"

"Why am I wearing the ring?"

"If he comes for me," Rowan said, his breath catching in his throat, "It won't be here. Loki would never think that I might hide his greatest desire right under his nose."

Ah, so she was a form of bait now. Normally she would have been offended, but right now she was far too tired to even think about it, much less muster anger. Behind her, Rowan's breathing slowed to gentle, even puffs against her neck, and she tried to relax against the sea of swirling thoughts. "There is something else," she said when she realized she couldn't contain it anymore.

"Mmm-hmm?" Rowan sighed, ruffling her hair with his breath.

"Loren…Loki," she corrected, "told me a story about a sword named Gram."

Rowan sat straight up in bed and reached for the lamp on the table. "What about it?"

"He called it the Dragon Slayer."

"Lily…" His voice was uneven, and his breathing oddly shallow. Lily's chest filled with dread. "What do you know of that sword?"

"Well…" She curled away from his hard stare. Her body sang with sudden tension, and she hated that she had to feel this way. She probably should have told him this sooner. "He said Loki wanted to own it. I thought he was just being eccentric at the time."

"Lily…" he repeated, his voice hard. She could hear the beginnings of that second timbre beneath it, and the sound frightened her.

"I think he has the sword…the real one." She blinked against the tears that squeezed out. "If all of this is real, I think Lor…Loki has the real sword. It has a black stain on the end that he swears is dragon's blood."

Rowan went still behind her. His breath stopped. Lily grew still as well, listening, afraid to turn and look at him. Tension filled the room, and had she not been terrified of his reaction, she would have slipped out of the bed and gone back to the guest room. For a long, strained moment, Lily believed coming to him was a mistake.

Just as she convinced herself that she needed to leave, his arms curled around her and she felt his lips against her shoulder. "Sleep, love," he whispered, sliding one hand under her cheek to turn her face up to his. He kissed her softly, his hands trembling with the effort, and pulled her tight against his chest. "Sleep now and we shall figure this out in the morning."

But sleep refused to come. No matter how she tried, Lily could not find the right combination of comfort and security to turn off the thoughts swirling in her head. Rowan held her close, his deep even breaths puffing against her neck in the darkness, and even that held no solace. Over and over she replayed the conversation, searching for anything to make the story less believable. The whole thing was pretty fantastic, but the seriousness and thinly-veiled panic etched into Rowan's features spoke volumes toward its truth.

When the alarm went off, she still hadn't slept. Reluctantly, she disentangled herself from Rowan's arms and padded down the hall toward the guest room and her things. If Rowan could smell Loki from that far away, she was willing to bet that Loki would be able to smell him all over her.

She showered and dressed, and was surprised to find Rowan waiting outside her door with a broad grin on his face. "Morning, beautiful," he said. The smile spread across her face before she knew it was there.

"Morning," she replied. "I thought since…well…" She felt the blush crawl up into her cheeks. Casting her gaze to his feet, Lily tucked stray, wet strands behind her ears. "I thought that if you could smell him out there last night, then he might smell you on me, and it might upset him."

Rowan chuckled as he closed the distance between them and kissed her soundly. Her back hit the wall as his tongue swept across hers and his hands traveled the length of her body. "God or not, this should make that stupid cat think twice about touching my woman," he growled when they separated.

His woman.

She liked that. Too much.

"I thought the point was to keep me safe, not make me a bigger target," she argued. Rowan caressed her face. She tilted her face up toward his. A small, thin smile tugged his lips upward.

"It is. Now he will know to keep you safe, or he will suffer the wrath of Asgard."

Lily rolled her eyes. "I have to go to work now." With a shrug, Rowan curled his arm around her shoulders and led her downstairs to where a car waited for her.

"Dane will let you off at the corner so you can walk in." There was a new sadness in Rowan's eyes as he kissed her forehead. "Be safe."

CHAPTER TWELVE

The morning was colder than usual. Every so often, small snowflakes floated past the car, and despite the toasty warmth of the car's interior, Lily shivered. She hadn't expected snow in November considering nature's threats of an Indian summer, yet here it was. As she stepped out onto the sidewalk, her foot slipped on the icy ground. For a moment she wasn't sure she would make it all the way to the door of the building, but after the initial adjustment in her balance and posture, she made it inside with no further problems.

Lily wasn't entirely sure what to expect when she pulled open the front door, but it certainly was not the warm and worried welcome she received. Loren—no, Loki, she reminded herself—swept her into a fierce hug. The tiny huff of expelled air was the only indication that something was wrong. Yesterday she would have allowed herself to enjoy this embrace. Now she looked at him not as an eccentric human, but as a cruel and calculating immortal. Loren was gone.

This man before her, embracing her, was something different and dangerous.

His name is Loki, she told herself. This new, enlightened image was not an attractive one. If she were honest with herself, she would have admitted that she was terrified of him.

"I was so worried about you," he cried as he released her. "I went by your house to check on you, but you weren't there. What on earth happened to you?"

"I stayed with a friend..." she said, as she shrugged out of her borrowed coat. Looking up, she met a concerned gaze from eyes that were a little too close to her own for comfort. "You two... my nerves were so rattled that I could barely sleep. Didn't you get my message?" His look of relief curled into a frown as he looked at his phone. Lily didn't buy it. He was a little too on-cue for any of it to be real. He knew. He had to know.

"Stupid technology," he said with a laugh. "I feel so silly now." Draping an arm around her shoulders, Loki towed her through the building to the storage room. She'd spent much time in there, and she knew the way. Something was wrong. First, he never would have met her at the door. Second, he was normally much too busy to walk her in. Lily glanced around the room, almost empty now, and bit back a sigh.

"I have to say," he said with great humor, "your interns take direction well. I went over to the gallery first thing this morning, and I'm impressed." Lily forced a smile in response, and shrugged out of his grip. Pulling a notebook from her bag, she focused her attention on it rather than him.

"They're good kids."

"Have you considered my offer?"

"Later, Loren." She wished he'd take the not-so-subtle hint and leave the room. After the previous night's revelations, she couldn't look at him without seeing lifetimes of cruelty and a month-long history of lies. There was a new coldness in his dark eyes that frightened her. She turned the page and marked through several lines of notes, then scribbled down the margin of the page. It was nonsense, really, but she hoped that appearing busy would run him off.

"Holy shit, there's an elephant in the room!" That got her attention. Groaning, Lily looked up to find him smiling at her. She scowled. "There's my girl."

"Not funny," she retorted. "Now kindly pick the canary feathers out of your teeth and go away."

"Maybe it isn't funny, but it is true." Loki laid his hand over hers to stop her. "What is it that we aren't talking about?"

Lily fixed him with a withering stare. She pulled her hand free, tucked her pen behind her ear, and crossed her arms over her chest. "Do you really want to do this?"

"We can't work like this, Lily."

"You mean I can't work like this. You're perfectly capable of making me insane with or without a problem."

Mischief crawled all over his features. "Come on, honey. Tell me what's going on."

"First, don't call me 'honey.' Second, I want to know why you and Rowan went all He-Man on each other last night." The air in the room grew noticeably cooler, even though his smile remained in place. "I don't want a ridiculous excuse either. I want the truth."

Loki considered her for a long, tense moment. She wondered how he would explain himself, wondered just how much of the truth she would get, and how much of what he would say matched what Rowan had already told her. She still didn't fully believe the story, but with every new twist, the fantastic seemed to focus more and more into the realistic. She also didn't believe that he would come out and announce his existence as a god from the Old World. Loki draped himself in Loren Eshu's familiar indifference and shrugged.

"I suppose the term 'mortal enemies' is the wrong one." *Yeah, you have to be mortal for that,* Lily thought. "He and I have orbited each other for years, as those with money are wont to do." Loki smirked as he leaned over the table toward her. "He's jealous that I'm more attractive than he is."

"Be serious." Her tone was flat, emotionless.

"We battle for the same artifacts. We tend to collect the same things." Lily leveled him with a hard stare that stopped him from saying more. She shivered again, wishing she hadn't taken her coat off and left it on the other side of the room.

"Did you know my past with him when you hired me?" Loki blinked, the only expression of surprise she'd seen cross his face since meeting him. "Before you answer, know that the continuation of whatever this relationship may or may not be depends on the answer to this question. So choose your words carefully."

Dust motes floated through the beams of light between them. Lily tensed, prepared to walk out when he hung his head.

"I knew he had interviewed you, yes," Loki admitted. "If you were enough to hold his attention and have him pull an advertisement, I thought it only right that I provide a little competition." He glanced up at her—the mischief was firmly back in place, twinkling in his eyes. "I never thought you would accept my offer."

Lily snapped her notebook closed and shoved it into her bag. He was absolutely insane. "Bullshit," she snarled. "Carolyn said you specifically requested me…and I know you well enough by now to know that you don't make offers without a guarantee that you will get what you want."

She slung her bag over her shoulder and headed for the door. Rage burned through her. She wanted to scream at him, to throw things and to completely undo an entire month of work. More than anything, she wanted away from him, as fast as possible. He blocked her exit by stepping in front of her. Lily bit back a curse and glared up at him.

"Where are you going?"

"To the gallery." She tried to go around, but he moved with her. The humor drained from his face. His mouth narrowed to a hard line, and the air around him dropped several degrees.

"What are you playing at?"

"Nothing." Lily tried to sound innocent, but her anger fused her jaw in place and she found it impossible to be nice. "I have work to do, and I don't want to do it around you."

"This is about Keir. You were with him."

"None of your business," she snapped. "You are my employer. There is no reason why I should tell you of my personal affairs." Fury flashed across his face. Lily closed her eyes and sucked in a deep, calming breath. "I need some time, Loren."

A long, tense moment held them locked in place. Loki's breath came in harsh, ragged puffs. This was a mistake. Lily knew that now. She'd come too close to the truth. He would surely kill her now. She waited, terrified and furious, until he let out a long sigh.

"Go." She opened her eyes and looked up to meet a cold, calculating stare. "But this is not over." He stepped back to allow her through, but caught her wrist in a steel grip. "Crossing me is a bad idea, Lily." Loki released her and strode off through the house.

Lily fled. She found herself standing on the sidewalk before she realized she had no transportation. And she left her coat inside.

Damn.

The gallery was eight blocks away. Normally she would walk, but not in this weather. And calling a cab could leave her standing there for much longer than it would take to walk. Frustrated, she plucked her phone from her bag and dialed the only number she could think of.

"What happened? What's wrong?" His worried voice washed over her, calming her nerves.

"I need a ride to the gallery. I left my coat inside and it's too cold to walk."

"I am right around the corner."

"Rowan…"

"You honestly did not think I would leave you alone with him, did you?"

She groaned. The chivalry, while oddly endearing, only reinforced the thought that she was up against something much too big, and her knight in shining armor was quite a bit more hairy than she wanted him to be. Lily started to answer, but she could already see his headlights coming around the corner. Sighing, she closed her phone and pulled the door open. Wondrous warmth blasted out to meet her.

"I should hate you," she grunted and flung herself down into the seat.

"Glad to see you too," Rowan replied, and leaned over to kiss her cheek before pulling away from the curb.

"This is beyond ridiculous."

"Why do you say that?"

"Because it is. Because you're hell-bent on protecting me, and that determination has made me even more of a target!" Rowan's features darkened. His foot fell heavy on the gas pedal, and the car shot forward through the intersection, making her clutch at the armrest. The muscle along his jaw began to tick.

"What did he say?" he asked through clenched teeth.

"Well...I asked him if his hiring me had anything to do with you." She rubbed her temples with her fingertips, trying to curb the headache behind her eyes. "He said he wanted a fair shot at me because I made you pull your ad."

"He knew it was mine?"

"Obviously, Rowan, or he wouldn't have said that."

Rowan swore, a long string of obscene words that made Lily blush. After several colorful phrases, he calmed himself, and sped past the gallery. Lily glanced back over the seat as her destination went whizzing by, and turned to him with an open-mouthed gawk.

"I need to see that book," he responded. "If it is what I think it is, then we may be in more trouble than I originally thought."

The house was cold, and the bitter, metallic smell of cat permeated the air, concentrated in the living room. A cold breeze drifted in from the back of the house. Rowan followed it, growling in frustration when he found the shattered window.

"He has been here," Rowan shouted back through the house. Immediately Lily was at his side, cowering under his arm. "Your home is no longer safe."

"I was afraid you were going to say that." She curled closer to his side. "He's been inside, hasn't he?"

"Yes."

"So…now what?" Her small body shook under his hands and he pulled her closer. She fit so well against his side. He couldn't imagine her not being there.

"Collect what you need. You will stay with me until this is over." Under his hand, her shoulders tensed. Stubborn woman. She still had no idea the danger she was in, and that blasted independent streak of hers was bound to get her killed.

"Here's the book." She offered it to him, and when his eyes found the worn cover, his heart seized in his chest. Plucking it from her fingers, Rowan turned it over in his hand. The familiar knotwork burned into its cover shook him. "Do you know it?"

Rowan swallowed around the lump in his throat. "It belonged to my father." Her big, blue eyes went wide and perfectly round.

"What…what does this mean?"

"Loki killed my father."

She gasped, and her arms went around his middle. He hugged her to him to stave off the shaking anger consuming him. "He was behind the death of my ancestors, which I knew all along. As far as my father's death, I have known it was by his hand for quite a long time. I just never had proof."

"And this journal…" she trailed off. Her eyes grew wide and perfectly round as realization hit. "Oh, Rowan…I'm so sorry."

"Do not be. I am very glad you found this." It gave him all the reason he needed to bring this war to a close. "Get your things. We need to go."

Lily scurried from the room. Rowan sank to the edge of the bed, cradling his head in one hand, the book clutched tightly in the other. He had known his father's death was at Loki's hands, but to have the proof was overwhelming. And now Lily was in danger. He'd been so selfish that he'd put the woman he loved in danger.

Rowan paused, feeling his eyebrows knit together. This was a new revelation. He loved her — probably the most irrational situation he had ever found himself in, but it was what it was. He loved her. He brought her into this. Now, he had to protect her.

Lily reappeared with a bag slung over her shoulder. She stood in the doorway with her arms wrapped around her middle. So small and vulnerable...the sight squeezed at Rowan's heart. He mentally kicked himself for being so stupid.

"I need to go to the gallery," she said. His guts twisted around themselves at the thought of putting her in such close proximity to his enemy. "I also need to return the book before he realizes it's gone." Rowan's hands tightened on the spine, making the old leather crackle. Lily noticed, because she laid her hands over his and spoke gently. "It may be your father's, but unless I take it back, we're going to have problems. If he was here, then he already knows I have it. I have to play dumb to save face."

She had a point, damn her. As much as it pained him to do so, Rowan loosened his grip on the book and let her slide it out of his hand. He knew she had to take it back. He only hoped she was as good an actress as she needed to be to get the ruse past the ultimate joker. Letting the book fall away, he wrapped his arms around her body and laid his head against her chest, pressing his ear to her skin to listen to her heartbeat. Strong and healthy. He only hoped he could keep it that way.

CHAPTER THIRTEEN

The gallery was bustling. Interns skittered from one end of the cavernous room to the other, sorting, repositioning, and squabbling over the general placement of items. With three days to go, the final shipments of restored pieces had arrived, and the rush toward the details was on. The scarcely-contained chaos was a nice change from the relative isolation of Loki's home. At least here she could feel the small swell of pride that came with a job well done. The show looked promising. She only hoped Loki would stay gone long enough to get setup finished.

No such luck.

As Lily settled herself into a corner and began to work on proper angling, Loki appeared on the opposite side of the room. His gaze immediately locked onto her. Lily's blood iced over, and despite the smile on his face she could see cold cruelty dancing in his eyes. The stolen book weighed heavily in the bag still slung around her body. Could he sense its presence?

That was ridiculous, yet as he ended his conversation and started toward her, Lily wasn't so sure. She tried to force a calm face as she reached into her bag and covertly snatched the book out. She dropped it onto the stack of books sitting on the table, and started flipping through the pages of the one open in front of her.

"What's that one?" Loki asked loudly enough for everyone to hear. "Looks like you brought it in yourself."

"A journal or...something," she stumbled, wrinkling her nose at the volume. "I borrowed it to read. I hope you don't mind."

"Not at all, sugar," he announced, then leaned forward. His nose almost touched hers. "Did you tell him everything you know?" he hissed. "Is the stupid dog ready to do this my way yet?"

She swallowed hard, hoping her surprise was genuine. "What? Who are you talking about?"

"Don't play stupid with me."

"I wouldn't have to if you'd just tell me what you're talking about." She turned her back to him, squeezing her eyes closed and counting to ten to calm her jangled nerves. She continued to flip through pages of the book in her hands. The old paper crackled, the spine threatening to come apart in her fingers, but even the familiar comfort of work could not erase the feeling of his icy glare from her back. "I have work to do...so if you plan to fire me, do it now."

Loki stilled behind her, then chuckled, a low, deep rumble in his chest that sounded entirely alien. "Oh, no. I'm not letting you get away that easily."

"Because for some stupid reason you see me as a bargaining chip." Lily scoffed. "You've build this ridiculous war around all of this stuff," she gestured to the room, "but you have no idea that I'm not one of your damn relics!" She wheeled around, stepping up into his face. "I'm not an object, Loren! I'm a person!"

Loki glared at her for another long moment before the serene, carefree face reappeared. His lips curled into a slow, knowing smile. He knew she was playing dumb, and for now it appeared he would play along.

"Well," he started, and laid his hand over hers. His fingers were ice cold. "I need to apologize to you. I was out of line."

Bullshit. She wanted to call him on it, bad idea as it might be. "I can't work for you full-time," she said instead. "Once the show is over, you'll have to find someone else."

"Don't leave me, Lily," he said, genuinely stricken. He looked almost panicked. "I will never find someone as good as you again." The transition in his demeanor was flawless. Well-rehearsed. But with just enough surprise that a small victory cry tried to rise from her throat. "At least let me take you to lunch and attempt to talk you into staying."

Bad idea, Lily, she told herself. Rowan wasn't going to like this, but she really had no way out. If things

201

were really serious enough to be classified as a war between them, she didn't have much choice but to play peacekeeper until she was out of the way.

"All right," she said, "but I have work to do first, so go away."

An hour and a half later, she sat across the table from Loki in a small diner. The place was worn and dingy, layered with years of hamburger grease and dust, but the people were friendly and kept to themselves. Lily felt isolated when he steered her into the corner, and now she sat trapped beneath his ever-shifting gaze. His eyes seemed to rotate colors as bright fluorescent lights flickered overhead. The room took on a surreal, nightmarish glow under the gloomy snow-day, and Loki reminded her of the swift and silent predator from the horror movies. Her heart thumped hard against her ribs. Every shred of consciousness screamed at her to run far and fast.

Lily knew she wouldn't make it to the door if she did. Loki was too smart, too fast.

"Why did you bring me here?" she asked, surprised by the steadiness in her voice. "Why even pretend to still be friends?"

"You are a great asset," he answered, and fixed her with his needling stare. "I may not approve of your choice of...friends," his face tightened and contorted, as if he were having a hard time holding the façade in place, "but sadly those decisions are not mine to make." The unspoken yet hung between them like dead weight. Something shifted across his cheekbones, and her stomach lurched in response. "I still want you...as more than just a curator."

"I don't understand why."

"You are intelligent and efficient...beautiful. I have been bewitched."

A bark of laughter erupted from her throat. She couldn't help it. Never in her life had she been accused of witchcraft, romantically or otherwise. "I'm sorry," she coughed as he narrowed his gaze in irritation, "I've never been told that before."

"It is the truth."

"I bet you say that to all the girls."

A familiar, thin smile curled his lips at their corners. "Perhaps. But what works on others seems lost on you."

"I'm not other women."

"Certainly not. Other women couldn't handle so much truth with such grace."

"So much truth?" She took a sip from her water glass. "What does that mean?"

"Don't insult your own intelligence." The same flash of cruelty she'd seen earlier fluttered in his visage. "You and I both know you aren't fooled by this show. You know it isn't friendly rivalry."

"Are you admitting that you want him dead?"

"Now why would I admit something like that?" His voice went light, airy. Loki leaned back and crossed his hands behind his head as he stared at the grimy ceiling. Lily followed his gaze up, her heart skipping a beat when she noticed the brown splotch on the sagging tile right above her. A leak—a bad one, by the look of it...and she was in the perfect position to be creamed by that tile, should it decide to say hello to the floor.

"Because it's easier than playing games," she said, watching the dubiously hanging tile. He chuckled. "But I forgot...playing games is what you do best."

"What makes you say that?"

"That's what a trickster does."

Loki dropped his hands and glanced around the room. When he snapped his fingers, everything around them froze.

She was a cheeky one, this little mortal.

She happily offered up all the proof he needed, too. It would be much easier to be himself and not continue with the human charade, yet it still seemed a shame to kill her. She was an attractive little thing, and likely great fun to take a romp with, but she was in the way...and the most precious thing in that damned dog's eyes.

Loki needed to wait. Taking her life would be the thing to distract Rowan, to give him the upper hand. He leaned forward, his body stretching and expanding as he rested his elbows on the table and looked down at her. Her shocked, horrified expression was absolutely priceless.

"Now listen closely." She swallowed, her throat bobbing with the effort. "The last place you want to be is in my way. I will have what is mine, one way or another."

"W-what does that have to do with me?" Ah, the poor, doe-eyed girl was afraid at last. Rightfully so... even if she wanted to put up that strong front.

"You may think you love your noble little wolf, but do not forget the guilt of his thieving ancestors." He watched her pulse flutter in her neck, and briefly considered how that rabbit-like beat would feel against his tongue. "I will have my ring back, and if you try to stop me, the force of the Valkyrie will not be able to save you."

The girl hesitated, only for a moment, but it was enough. "I don't know what you're talking about," she lied. She could act, he'd give her that. But her little show would only get her deeper in trouble if she didn't put an end to it.

"Of course you do, Lily. I don't have to explain it all to you again." He picked up his tea glass and took a long drink. One thing the deep south had over Asgard was this. Even Mimir's Well of Wisdom paled in comparison. "You have a choice. You can stay away from the dog, and out of my way—join me, if you wish it so. Or, you can die alongside him."

Lily's mouth fell open in horror as she stared up at his enlarged form. She wondered briefly what he really looked like without facades. The thought was quickly squelched by the more pressing ultimatum.

Join him or die? Really?

She wasn't ready to shuffle off her mortal coil just yet, but she knew she didn't want to turn her back on Rowan. Loren—no, Loki—would no doubt protect her and devote himself to her, at least until he tired of her. Until she grew too old to keep his ageless attention. But Rowan...every time she looked at him she saw the future reflected in his eyes. Loki was right. She did love her noble wolf.

The ring, until that moment forgotten on the chain around her neck, weighed heavily against her chest. She hadn't asked what the ring's power was, and she didn't want to know now. All she knew was that it being so close to this creature was a dangerous game to play, but a powerful chip. The last place he would think to look would be on her person. At least, she hoped that was his logic.

"How long do I have to decide?" she asked. Exasperation greeted her. Good to know she could keep him on his toes.

"Twenty-four hours," he said on a sigh. "A simple yes or no will suffice."

"Your way or no way, right?"

He grinned, his too-straight, too-white teeth glittering in the dull diner light. "Precisely." He raised his hand and snapped his fingers. The activity in the room resumed without so much as a misstep, but Loki was nowhere to be seen. Several bills lay on the table next to his untouched plate. She could almost feel the rotation of the earth beneath her, and for several moments she was certain she would vomit.

Things like this weren't supposed to happen to people like her. Ancient gods didn't just stop time to make threats and then vanish in her world. Of course, men didn't turn into wolves at will either, but she chose to ignore that facet of reality for the time being. Speaking of shape-shifting men…

Lily snatched her phone out of her purse, dialed his number, and fell apart when he answered.

"Lily, where are you?" Rowan asked, but the heaving sobs coming through the earpiece drowned out his words. "Babe, you have to calm down and talk to me. What happened?"

The sounds grew stifled, and after a moment, slowed. She sniffled, then coughed. "H-he...he..."

"Did he hurt you?"

A pause. "No."

"Tell me where you are."

"The...the café on...on 60th and Habersham..."

Rowan swore under his breath. "I am on my way. Is he still there?"

"No."

"Tell me what happened."

"I...don't know." She sniffled, and the sound of ice rattling in a glass echoed through the phone. When she spoke again, her voice was steadier. "He just...vanished."

Rowan ran a red light, narrowly avoiding a collision with a recycling truck, and bit back a snarl. She was alone, a bare minimum of ten minutes away from him. Loki could come back at any time, and as anyone. The thought raced through his mind and chilled him to the core. He dropped his foot on the gas pedal, taking the corner of Calhoun Square fast enough to threaten two wheels. The car skidded on the icy road, then the treads bit and righted. Rowan exhaled heavily.

"I will be there as soon as I can," he said. "I want you to keep talking to me."

"About what?"

"Tell me what happened after I dropped you off at the gallery." A car stopped to turn left in front of him, blocking his passage. He punched the steering wheel in frustration.

"Rowan…" She sounded tired.

"Please, Lily. Just keep talking. Tell me everything."

She did. The more she talked, the steadier her voice grew. She recounted every moment up to and including Loki's vanishing act. Rowan rounded cars on the wrong side of the road, cut down two one-way streets going the wrong way, slipped and slid on un-scraped side streets, and shot down Habersham Street at breakneck speed. The tires squealed and crunched on ice and salt as he pulled into the loading area at the shop-front and threw on his flashers, but before he could turn to open his door, Lily was in the car with her arms around his neck.

"I have you." Those three words were quite possibly the most profound ones she'd ever heard. His strong arm went around her body, crushing her to him like a steel band. Rowan peppered her cheek and forehead with kisses. "I have you," he repeated. Lily formed herself against him, letting the feeling of safety crawl through her.

"What do we do?" she asked when she trusted herself to speak again.

"We end this, one way or another."

"He wants to kill you."

"He has tried for centuries. It has not worked yet, has it?" Lily released her choke-hold on him and sank back into the seat. The dreary day outside the car seemed to have intensified while she wasn't looking. "We need to get out of here," Rowan suggested, and she nodded.

Lily couldn't remember the last time she'd seen snow in Savannah. Huge, white chunks fluttered on the breeze as Rowan maneuvered the car back onto the highway toward his home. She wondered if Loki had anything to do with the sudden seasonal reversal and shivered. If he had the power to change the weather…

"Are you cold?" Rowan asked, already reaching for the controls. Lily shook her head.

"Just…remembering." His hand changed direction and landed on her leg, just above her knee. "He wants me to join him, or he'll kill me."

"So you said." Rowan's voice sounded strange. Flat. Emotionless. "But that will not happen," he said emphatically.

"How can you be sure of that?" He answered her with a hard glance. "Damn it, Rowan. He's a god! He can't be killed and he has unimaginable power!"

"Even gods have their weaknesses, Lily."

The only thing that tempts him is…" Lily bit her lip. "…treasure."

"Anything of value to another." He smirked. "He wants you because I do."

"Then if you no longer want me…"

"No." His hand tightened on her leg.

"Rowan…"

"No. I will not have him near you again." She snatched his hand away from her and threw it back toward him.

"Stop trying to be so damned noble and listen to me." She dragged a deep breath through her nose, willing herself not to scream at him. "If I go to him willingly…tell him you and I fought and you tossed me out…then I'm not a threat anymore. I can collect information that might help you."

"If he catches you, he will kill you," he growled.

"A chance I have to take." Lily leveled him with a hard look. Rowan appeared ready to argue more, but her mind was made up. Defeat registered in his features.

"So I've lost you."

Lily fought the urge to groan and took his hand. "No. We just need to make him think you have." They stopped at a red light, and she reached out to turn his face toward hers. "You can't protect me and end this at the same time." She stroked her thumb over his full bottom lip, smiling at its softness. "Let me worry about me right now."

He pursed his lips and kissed the pad of her thumb, then turned his face into her hand and kissed her palm. "I do not like this. At all."

"Me either. But this is my only option." The light changed. They lapsed into silence, but Rowan held onto her hand as they made the slow trek back to his home. With Chatham Square closed by an accident, the drive was extended, then halted completely by traffic. Lily took the opportunity to get more information. "How do you plan to end this?"

"Kill him." His voice was like steel. Her mouth fell open.

"If the other gods couldn't accomplish that, how do you expect to do it?"

He smirked. "That, my love, is the part I have not yet figured out."

CHAPTER FOURTEEN

Lily tossed and turned in the darkness. Sleep evaded her despite the bottle of wine and two rounds of intense lovemaking they had shared. Beside her, Rowan's deep, even breaths echoed in the darkness, giving her little distraction. She couldn't seem to wipe from her mind the look of fury Rowan showed when they discussed her plan.

You do know he will expect more than a platonic relationship, he'd reminded her. She knew. Though she wasn't thrilled by the prospect of letting Loki — or Loren, whichever he chose to be — paw her like a high-school freshman at his first party, she was willing to sacrifice a little of her dignity for the cause.

Just not all of it.

Her heart belonged to Rowan. After his statement in the car, she knew it. The moment he uttered that small reassurance, she fell completely and irrevocably in love with him. And while she knew that would not change, she also knew the unspoken truth between them.

That her boss and soon-to-be Lord and Master would expect much more than a kiss or some heavy petting. As his underling, he would expect everything she had to offer, and would take it without hesitation. Lily couldn't give him that. And in denying him, Loki would understand the ruse.

She flipped over again, and jumped when she looked directly into Rowan's sparkling, and mildly worried, eyes.

"I thought I had sufficiently worn you out," he muttered, his sleepy voice full of gravel. "I suppose I did not do it right."

"You did," she reassured him, and her insides gave a little shiver of pleasure as she thought about it. "But my brain still has adrenaline to burn." Rowan opened his mouth in a deep yawn, then reached out and towed her across the bed to him. Lily snuggled down against his chest, enjoying his warmth.

"Worrying tonight will not help you tomorrow, my love."

"Can't help it."

"Just because I hate your plan does not mean I do not think it is a good one."

"I just hope I can follow through."

His chest rumbled with laughter. She crushed her ear to his skin, listening. "Sleeping with the enemy is a daunting task, is it not?"

"Who says I will be sleeping with him?"

SIOBHAN KINKADE

Rowan stilled, his breath a near-imperceptible huff against the top of her head. "You know —"

"I'm choosing not to think about it," she cut him off, her voice flat. "Hopefully you will figure this out before I have to resort to that."

"Me?"

"Yeah, you. You're the grand strategist. I'm just the decoy."

Rowan laughed again, and kissed the top of her head. "You are quite the beautiful distraction. I will give you that." He squeezed her, his arms threatening to pop bones as he did. "With you around, Loki may just forget about the ring." Releasing her, Rowan gently brushed her hair back from her face. "Sleep now." His fingertips traced lazy circles up and down her spine. "We can sort it all out in the morning."

"Maybe you should take the ring back and hide it," she murmured as he lulled her back toward sleepiness.

"The last place Loki will think to look is right under his nose. Just promise me you will not give it to anyone if they ask...not even me."

"Why would I not give it to you?" Lily leaned up to look at him, but he tucked her back down under his arm.

"Just do this for me, please." She nodded against his chest. Lily still had more to say, but it was lost as she slipped into unconsciousness.

At nine o'clock sharp, Lily stood in the gallery, sleepy, and looking at her handiwork. She'd grudgingly risen at six-thirty to scrub herself clean, then slipped away from Rowan's questing grasp with the promise to call him every chance she got. The ring still hung on the chain around her neck, and she prayed Loki wouldn't notice it.

He still had yet to put in an appearance this morning. That suited her just fine, but the anticipation racing through her was sheer misery. He did tell her he would give her twenty-four hours, but she didn't want to wait to give him the news. Seeing that the interns had the details under control, she slipped out of the gallery and found a quiet stairwell. Lily lowered herself to a cold, concrete step and dialed Loki's telephone number.

"I assume you have an answer." Right to the point. She had to admire that about him.

"I do."

"I'm on my way." The line went dead before she could reply, and by the time she closed the phone he was sitting on the step next to her. His sudden appearance caused her to jump, and she covered her mouth with one hand to stifle a surprised shriek.

"First," she snapped when she could breathe again, "don't ever do that to me again." He brought his fist to his chest and bowed slightly.

"My apologies." Loki straightened, the thinnest of smiles on his lips. "You were going to tell me something."

"I am, but I need to preface this conversation by saying that I am not some waif you can throw around at will. You are not in the Old Country anymore, and Asgard's rules do not apply in the modern world. You have to respect my boundaries."

"Fair enough."

"Yes, I have a history with Rowan."

"Understood."

"He is part of my past."

Loki raised one curious eyebrow at her. "Is he now?"

"Leave him alone," she said sharply. Lily fixed him with a hard stare and fought the urge to wither as he held her gaze. "He is of no consequence to you. You have me. You win. Now leave it." His lips curled in a way that reminded Lily of the Grinch from the old Dr. Seuss cartoon. His eyes cycled through colors, and some small, nearly imperceptible thing changed about him. Lily swallowed.

"You see, that is entirely untrue." His voice shifted again, into that strong, almost regal sound that frightened her. "The dog has something that belongs to me, and until I get it back and the dragon's bloodline is no more, I will continue to hunt him."

Lily fought hard to rein in her terror. "Even if you had this proverbial ring, you would still kill him?"

"You are no longer with him, Lily. What does it matter?"

"Killing people is wrong, you idiot!" she shrieked, and rose to her feet. "You can't just go around destroying people you don't like!"

"Watch. Your. Tongue."

Lily blinked, and let the anger rise. "No," she snarled. "I will not watch my tongue just to satisfy your foolish pride. God or not, you live as a man and you damn well better start acting like one, or I'm done with both of you." She turned on her heels and stalked across the small landing toward the door. "I have work to do. You and I will discuss this later, when I'm not quite so ready to throttle you."

"I would much like to see you try," he replied, and his laughter followed her back into the gallery before the door could slam on it.

Growling, Lily snatched her phone out of her pocket and shot off a quick text message to Rowan.

He's absolutely insufferable. Don't know if I can do this.

Deleting the evidence of her lie, she stuffed the phone back into its place and grabbed her clipboard from her bag. Two days to go, and things were already perfect. Her interns were doing little more than polishing cases and adjusting the case lights to better showcase each item. Her heart jumped into her throat when she looked above the far wall to see the huge sword hanging on a plaque, its sharp blade still coated in black. She had no doubt now that it was everything he'd accused it of being, and possibly more. And as she stared at it, and glanced around at the rest of the collection, she realized that she had just spent the last month single-handedly restoring the private arsenal of a god. Scattered between the weapons were pieces of gold in the form of goblets, jewelry, scepters, and various other tidbits the kings of lore had died for.

And she realized another thing. Loki already had the majority of the treasure. But…how did he get it? Snatching her phone back from her pocket, she shot off a second message.

Loki has the treasure?

The time lag between that message and Rowan's response seemed endless.

Parts of it. Stole it years ago. Wants the ring.

She already knew that. And she also knew that if he wanted Rowan dead, any one of the items she'd meticulously cleaned, catalogued, and displayed could easily do it. Lily felt sick. Regardless of whether Loki—Loren—whatever his name was—caught her, she grabbed her phone and fired off another message to Rowan.

Restored his arsenal. He wants to kill you. What do we do?

Within seconds, the light on her phone winked at her, and she read his reply.

End this. Opening is Saturday. He will not risk losing face in front of others. Stay safe.

Rowan stared at the messages Lily had sent. His blood was near boiling in his veins. Loki had her, he had the sword and the majority of the treasure, and the ring was within arm's reach… but the one thing Rowan had over him?

Determination.

And an absolute lack of desire to own the damned ring. Keeping it out of Loki's hands was the most important task…the only true reason for his existence. Rowan trusted Lily not to fail him—her heart was pure, and he had faith that she would do the right thing when she needed to.

She said he had an arsenal. No doubt Loki would collect weaponry. Likely tokens of affection from his followers, or maybe battle trophies of deceased foes. Either way, Rowan knew he was in for a fight. But that fight could very well be the end of him. He needed to get his mind off of Lily, and to worry about the task at hand.

Let me worry about me.

He promised her he would focus, but his focus had narrowed to only include her, and so long as she was in direct danger, there was little he could do in the way of planning to take down an old god.

"Dane!" Rowan shouted. Within moments, his assistant appeared and Rowan bit back a smile, remembering how Lily gave a delicate shudder and called him Lurch when they last spoke of him. "I need a ticket to the Gallery opening on Friday."

"Yes, sir."

"And Dane?"

"Sir?"

"Lighten up. You are too much like Lurch." For the first time that Rowan remembered, the young man cracked a smile.

"Your ticket is already on your desk," he replied. "I ordered it last week." The small smile turned into a broad grin as he turned and walked away. Rowan only shook his head. He was nothing if not efficient.

Now that he'd secured passage, he just had to figure out exactly how he would go about separating Loki's head from the rest of him.

"Have dinner with me tonight." His voice so close behind her nearly caused Lily to drop her clipboard.

"I already told you not to sneak up on me," she said through gritted teeth. She sighed and turned to face him. "Do I really have any other option?"

"Not really. However, you get to decide where we go." Lily briefly considered looking up the most expensive restaurant in Savannah just to exact a bit of childish revenge, but her conscience refused to allow it. He would surely expect repayment in some form. Instead, she shrugged.

"Surprise me," she offered. He smiled again, but it didn't touch his eyes the way Rowan's did. Her gut twisted.

"Oh, I'm full of surprises." He closed the distance between them with two steps and tipped her head back to brush a soft kiss across her lips. Shudders of repulsion hovered just beneath the surface of her skin. "But you already knew that." How someone so cold could be so tender amazed her, and she hated him for it. Behind her, the college kids working for her hooted and catcalled. Lily's face flamed. She felt his influence tugging on her mind, wanting her to fall into him, to accept him. "You blush so beautifully, Lily," he whispered, "I wonder if you turn pink all over."

CHAPTER FIFTEEN

Rowan was waiting just inside the living room when Lily got home. Without a word, he crossed the room, pulled her into his arms, and kissed her roughly. Again he tasted like whiskey, and the wicked way his tongue danced across hers reminded her of all the wonderful, depraved things he could do with it. Rowan crushed her body to him, claiming her with enough force to make her squeak in discomfort.

"I apologize," he said as he broke away. "But I cannot bear the thought of you being with him." Lily wrapped her arms around him and laid her head against his chest.

"It has to be this way."

"I still hate it."

"I do too, but he'll be here to pick me up for dinner soon, and if he catches you here he'll kill both of us."

Rowan sighed, long and loud. He cradled her face in his hands and looked deep into her eyes. Lily swore he could see her very soul. Her mind momentarily flat-lined. All she could think about was him. The way he smelled. The feel of his hands on her skin.

The warmth radiating from him. The memory of him moving inside her.

"I hate this, Lily."

"I know."

"I do not want to let you go with him."

"The sooner you end this, the less time I'll have to be with him."

"I know."

Sighing, Lily pushed up on her toes and kissed him. His arms went around her waist again, and he crushed her close, molding her form to him as his hands traveled from her shoulders down around her rear. Lily let him hold her close while she drew his tongue into her mouth and suckled it gently. When she finally took his face in her hands and pulled back, they were both breathless.

"We have to stop," she gasped, and carefully disentangled herself from his grasp. "As much as I want to keep you, you need to go and I need to get ready."

Rowan groaned. "I know," he said. He sounded so heartbroken. Her chest ached for him.

"End this," she said, and squeezed his arm as she passed by and locked herself into the bathroom. As she started the shower, she heard the faint click of the back door closing. Lily blinked back tears as she climbed under the hot stream and washed away his scent from her body.

The dog had been here. Recently. Despite her best efforts to remove it, his stink still permeated the air. In the back of the house, the washing machine ran. Windows stood open despite the bitter cold and melting icicles hanging from the eaves. The window had already been replaced. The house smelled of winter and strawberries, and he knew by the sound of her feet on the carpet that she was stalling. Lily was always efficient to a fault. She never took extra time to do something.

"Everything okay?" he called out, and heard the soft thump of something hitting the floor.

"Coming!" she shouted back, and he picked up on the low curse she muttered. As she scurried up the hall, Loki considered his options. He should cut his losses and kill her now. He should…but the temptation to cut her pretty little throat in front of the wolf was still too strong. She would be the tool he needed to bring Keir to his knees and give up the treasure once and for all.

Plus, the temptation to strip her of her dignity as well as her clothing was ever-present. Debauchery with her would be the ultimate insult to the wolf. And, Loki really did want to know if she flushed all over when something knocked her off balance.

His eyes sparkled like they were imbedded with a thousand tiny jewels. Lily gave a delicate shiver as she crossed the room and painted a too-broad smile on her face.

"I'm sorry about that," she said, her voice too airy, too bright.

"What kept you?"

"Oh…my mom called," she lied. He didn't buy it—she knew that—but said nothing.

"I hope she's well." He offered his arm. "Dinner awaits." Reluctantly, Lily accepted his outstretched elbow and allowed him to lead her to the car. He smelled nice, and he was attractive enough, but the thrill of his company was nothing. Desire didn't whip through her at the sight of him. He didn't fuel her imagination the way Rowan did. When Loki wasn't around, it was easy to tell herself she could allow him the things he wanted, but in his presence she knew that was never going to happen.

She only hoped she could use his intimidating nature and a little ego-stroking to throw him off.

Naturally, Loki chose the most expensive restaurant in the whole of Savannah. Lily wanted to groan, but she knew there would be no benefit in it. Be strong, she reminded herself, and stepped onto the sidewalk. Lily and Loren — at least, what she pretended was Loren — lapsed into a tense silence as they took their seats in a remote corner of the restaurant. Around them, the low hum of contented diners filled the air. Glasses and silverware clinked. Linens rushed against legs and chairs. The soft churn of the old building's furnace filled the space between silence and sound. Lily folded her hands in her lap and stared at her wine glass. The liquid inside looked like blood.

"This isn't working, is it?" Lily asked. Across the table, Loki remained immobile.

"I am afraid it isn't."

"Well, you didn't give me much choice, you know." She accented the sentence with a pointed look over the lip of her glass. "Besides, this time yesterday you stopped time and gave me an ultimatum. Forgive me for being tense," she growled. He smiled. It made her want to slap him.

"Self preservation is a strong motivator."

"It is," she agreed, reining in her anger. "It's the only thing keeping me in this chair."

"He came to see you today."

"He did. I told him that it was over."

"Keir doesn't take hints well."

"No, but I think he values his life enough that he won't be any more trouble for you."

"So long as he breathes, he will be trouble for me."

Their dinner appeared, halting their conversation. Lily had no appetite, and found she could only push her dinner around her plate. Loki ate as if he hadn't a care in the world.

"One of the things I have come to appreciate about the modern world is the cuisine," he said between bites. "Indefinite existence is made much better by the addition of a good meal."

"You have these powers," Lily said, shifting the conversation again. "Why not just stop time and take the ring."

Loki shrugged. "Where's the sport in that?"

"This is all a game to you…"

"Of course."

"You are absolutely insufferable," she snapped. He paused, his features twisting back into Loki's cruel façade.

"You would do well to watch your tongue, girl."

"Perhaps," she pushed her plate away, "but maybe my sense of self-preservation isn't as strong as you thought." His expression darkened. "Don't expect me to immediately fall at your feet or into your bed. Just because I made the choice to come to you does not mean you have me."

"Then why come to me at all?"

"Consider it a peacekeeping mission."

"Just understand, Lily," he hissed, dropping his fork to his plate. He dropped his elbows to the table and steepled his hands in front of his face. "I always get what I want, one way or another."

Lily lay awake in bed, thoughts tumbling through her mind so fast that she could remember few of them even seconds after they passed. Despite the tumult, she was acutely aware of two things:

1. She missed Rowan.
2. She was terrified of Loki.

As if reading her mind, the phone on the nightstand rang. Without looking at the caller ID, not with a greeting, but with his name.

"Rowan?"

"Gods, Lily…I cannot do this."

"Do what?"

"Stay away from you."

Lily sighed, warmed by the sentiment. "I don't want to, but you know we have to."

"One way or another, this will be over in forty-eight hours." His voice held a hard edge; a promise.

"I hope so."

Rowan paused, his breath rasping into the phone for several long moments. "I love you, Lily."

Her heart stuttered, then seemed to expand in her chest. A broad smile split her face even as tears

229

threatened to fall. "I love you, too," she replied, her voice scarcely above a whisper.

"Sleep well."

"Good night."

Lily slept after that, though not well, and not for long. The alarm went off at six-thirty, and she grudgingly dragged herself from the warmth of her bed. One more day, and the show would be underway. And soon enough, this madness could come to its long-awaited end.

CHAPTER SIXTEEN

"What?"

Lily blinked at the watery-eyed kid in front of her. He looked like he would piss himself if she made any sudden movements.

"Miss Reynolds came through about ten minutes ago and said we were going to open tonight." With a defeated sigh, Lily sank onto a nearby bench. "Sorry, Lily," the kid offered before scurrying away.

She scrubbed her face with her palms and tried to swallow the panic in her throat. She needed to talk to Carolyn and fast. She struggled to her feet and ran for the stairwell. Taking two steps at a time, Lily burst through the fourth-floor door and into the sterile office.

"What do you mean we open tonight?" she shrieked by way of introduction. "We aren't ready!"

"Of course you are," Carolyn said without so much as batting an eyelash. "Your interns are buffing fingerprints from cases. And Mr. Eshu—"

"Is completely insane!" she shouted. "You can't do this to me!"

"Oh, but I can." Loki's smooth, cold voice startled her. "It is, after all, my collection."

"Why?" she snapped, rounding on him. "Why change it now?"

"Your work is magnificent," he said, moving close up behind her. She could feel the warning in his words. "I want to change it now because you have given me such a spectacular display that I can't wait to get started."

Lily wished they weren't having this conversation here. At all, actually. But there wasn't much room for wishes anymore.

"Fine," she said through gritted teeth. "Tonight." She had to talk to Rowan…soon. She hoped his plans could be moved up too. Another bolt of terror rushed through her—did Loki know of Rowan's plans? Was that why he moved things up? "If we have to open tonight, then I need to get back to work."

"A word first?" Loki asked.

"Later. I'm busy." Rude? Certainly. But Lily couldn't be bothered to give a damn. He'd already inconvenienced her enough. If he was determined to talk again, he would have to follow her and make her talk. She raced from the room, slamming open the stairwell door, where she pulled out her phone.

Opening moved up. Gala tonight.

Less than a breath later, it blinked.

Loki is onto us. Will move fast. Be prepared and be careful.

Lily hurtled herself down the stairs and back to the gallery. Four interns stood in the middle of the room, whispering amongst themselves, unaware of her presence. When one saw her, each of them straightened and turned to face her.

"We're opening tonight," Lily said on a sigh. "We have to be ready. I'm sure we are, but let's go over things one more time."

Together, Lily and her army of frizzy-haired, freckled college kids spent the afternoon perfecting their work; reanalyzing, re-tagging, and re-cleaning. Finally, at 4:30 she sent them home and made her last pass before turning for the door.

Loki blocked her path.

"I think you and I will talk now."

"If you insist," she said in a flat tone.

"Watch your tongue, girl."

"What do you want?" she asked with a derisive snort.

"Tonight," he said, advancing on her, "you will appear as my escort." She stood her ground, even as he stood so close that their bodies touched. "And you will be my lover."

"But I'm not."

"You will be."

"You said—"

"I know what I said," he snorted. "But you would do well to remember that I do not make a habit of keeping trivial promises." With a sudden rush of fear, Lily backed away several steps.

233

"God or not, you'd do well to keep this one," she said, and fled the building. She expected to find him blocking her path, but he never appeared. She reached her car, frightened and gasping for breath, and tore away from the building before remembering the icy roads and her not-so-new tires.

Cursing herself, Lily righted her car on the road and focused on getting home alive, which seemed to help alleviate the raw fear from Loki's last few statements. The words still bounced through her brain, but she had more important things to worry about…like getting home in one piece and getting back. The majority of the snow was gone, but the water left in its place was already starting to ice over again, making the roads even more dangerous. Combining that with the wet southern air, Lily feared the condition of the roads as the day grew later.

At the same time, she had to wonder how on Earth they had moved the gala in only a few minutes. Two thoughts crossed her mind simultaneously. First, they'd been working on it for weeks and hadn't told her. Why they wouldn't give her notice, she didn't understand. Second, she was dealing with an old god. He could do almost anything he wished. He'd likely stopped time again or gone back and changed events as he saw fit, particularly if he knew she wasn't one-hundred percent on his side.

She only hoped as she navigated the slick streets into her neighborhood that Rowan still had enough time to concoct his plan.

Lily was careful to lock both the front door and the bathroom door behind her before she shucked her clothes and stepped into the calming heat of her shower. Over and over her mind replayed the wicked things she and Rowan had done in the small space, which didn't help her nerves.

It was with shaking hands that she fastened the zipper on her dress and twisted her hair into the smooth chignon that bared her neck and the chain holding the ring. She had grown so used to its cold weight around her neck that she'd managed to forget about it.

Lily's first thought was to take it off — to bury it in her jewelry box and let it wait out this madness. But even as she reached for the clasp she found she couldn't. Instead, she stared at her reflection and the gold band lying just at the curve of her breasts, contemplating her options.

She only had one... Wear it. She was already damned. She may as well let Loki know she had what he wanted. With one final deep breath, Lily fluffed her bangs and left the house.

Once again Rowan found himself pacing the house like a caged animal. Damn Loki. Once again he'd found a way to be two steps ahead. Unfortunately, Lily's life hung in the balance, and that said nothing at all of her dignity. Loki would no doubt take what he wanted, whether or not she was willing to give it. He'd find a way to twist her brain and make her think it was him that she wanted.

Snarling, Rowan punched the wall, putting a six-inch dent in the plaster and drywall in the shape of his fist.

His best tuxedo hung over the back of the bathroom door, freshly laundered and pressed. Luckily Dane was efficient, whether he smiled or not, and Rowan had everything he needed to end this. Or so he hoped.

He didn't have the massive arsenal Loki possessed. He didn't have the god's cunning wit and timeless wisdom. But he had seen Asgard, sipped from the Well of Wisdom, and lived more than half a century while watching those he loved wither and die around him. And now the one person that could change his very existence was trapped at the heart of the threat. The task passed down to him by blood stood unfinished, and no matter what it took—a shift or a sharp-edged blade—this would end tonight.

Rowan stripped out of his clothes and stepped into the tux, careful to knot the tie just the right way, line up the cummerbund with maniac precision, and brush the two bits of lint from the left sleeve of the coat. He stepped into his shoes, and on the way out the door picked up the keys to his car. His last option was to choose a weapon at the door and hope like hell it was the right one.

Despite the sudden change in date, the gallery was packed. Men and women in their most fashionable southern-socialite attire milled around the museum, their eager eyes cast toward the still-closed French doors. A large, red ribbon stretched across them. The air was light, expectant. All of these people, she thought, so oblivious to the truth. She understood now the phrase "ignorance is bliss." The toughest decision most of these people were faced with in the past twenty-four hours was what to wear to this very function.

Loki moved among the crowd with grace and ease. Many people called to him by name, while every other person in receipt of his attentions fawned under his gaze. His façade was flawless...except those eyes. Those dark orbs reflected cunning and cruelty, and when they located Lily, the gaze that followed chilled her blood. The ring hung like dead weight around her neck. She realized something as he crossed the room toward her. She was terrified. She had no idea

LOKI'S GAME

how to proceed. The plan was all in Rowan's head, and she wasn't privy to that information.

"You look stunning," Loki said, and pulled her against him. Lily silently prayed he wouldn't notice the ring as he tipped her chin up and brushed his lips over hers.

"Thank you," she replied, disentangling herself from his arms. "Excuse me. I have to go open the gallery." She tried to smile at him, and had no idea if she succeeded. "We'll talk in a minute, okay?" She turned away and raced toward the ribbon-wrapped doors leading to the exhibit. Loki fell into step several paces behind her and she tried not to focus on his overwhelming presence.

As she turned to face the chattering crowd, a wave of panic crashed over her. She *hated* large groups. Loki watched her with an expression of amusement. She wanted to punch him.

"Ladies and gentlemen," Lily shouted, but only a few patrons even acknowledged her. "May I have your attention please!" she tried again, to no avail.

A sharp, piercing whistle echoed through the building, immediately silencing the crowd. Everyone turned toward her, and Loki winked as he slipped his fingers from his mouth. "All yours," he whispered.

"Thanks," she replied, and turned a smile toward the crowd. "Thank you all for coming," she said, and prayed her voice remained steady. "The exhibit inside is truly a fascinating one. Spanning history, from the

238

dawn of time through the present, the artifacts you will see tonight are of the highest quality and rarest form. Some of the items contained inside are even rumored to have been owned by gods themselves." A chuckle rippled through the crowd. "This evening, and this wonderful feature would not be possible without the kindness and generosity of one of the Gallery's most affluent benefactors, Mr. Loren Eshu."

The crowd clapped, though the sound reminded her more of boredom than gratitude. Loki smiled and waved his hand.

"Thank you," he said, and at the back of her consciousness, Lily felt the tug of his influence. "But I refuse to take the credit for this show. Four weeks ago, Miss Redway came into my home and faced an unbelievable challenge. The items in the room behind me were packed away in boxes, crammed in corners, and generally neglected. In a stunning display of concentration, talent, and intuition, she has, in just under a month, mind you, turned my haphazard collection of junk into a showcased display of history that any collector could be proud to call his own." He curled one arm around her waist and pulled her close. "Thank you, Lily, for all of your hard work." Bending at the waist, Loki pressed his lips to her cheek, and whispered in her ear. "If you try anything, you will be the villain in this room."

Lily swallowed, beat back the panic, and grinned broadly at him as he righted himself. "Now why would I do something like that?" she asked under her breath as the noise subsided. "Thank you," she responded to the uneager applause. "As you move through the exhibit, please be sure to speak to the attendants. As interns, they…" she faltered as a new presence overtook her senses.

Rowan.

She felt him long before he entered the room, and found it hard not to physically react to his presence. He was calming and invigorating and reassuring and unbalancing all at the same time, and she had to shake herself to regain her train of thought.

"I'm sorry," she said with a nervous chuckle, "I wandered off there for a moment." The crowd chuckled as well which, thankfully, put her at ease. "As I was saying, they have done the majority of the grunt work, and are eager to share their progress with you. They are extraordinary young men and women, and I could not have done it without them." She picked up the over-sized scissors from the podium and turned to Loki, using the moment to gauge his reaction to Rowan's presence.

Loki had completely shut down. His dark eyes were cold and empty. No humanity remained in his demeanor, and when she pushed the scissors into his hand, he did not respond.

"Take it," she ordered. Only then did his gaze flicker to her. "Wait until they're inside," she added. Loki took the comical shears from her and, smoothing his features into the serene mask he'd worn earlier, turned to the doors.

"It is with great pleasure that I present to you my personal collection: Shadows of History." He slipped the blades over the ribbon and snipped it in two. Another round of applause, more enthusiastic this time, rose as he pushed open the doors and waved the patrons inside. In the rush he reached out and pulled Lily flush against his side. She squeaked in surprise, but managed to keep her smile painted across her lips.

She dared a glance around, but Rowan was nowhere to be seen. He was still close; she could feel him out there.

"Don't try anything," Loki snarled in her ear. Lily sighed.

"I have an exhibit to run," she snapped, and pulled loose from his grip. He allowed her to move, but caught her wrist and turned her back toward him.

"Remember, girl, you came to me."

"Yes, I remember."

"If you get in my way, I will kill you too."

"Funny," she mused, and smirked at him as she ripped loose from his grasp, "I thought you were planning to do that anyway."

CHAPTER SEVENTEEN

Loki was pissed off. Rowan had at least managed to accomplish that much by showing his face. Granted, such action could very well have put Lily in even more danger, but it had to be done. He only hoped Lily could run crowd control while he slipped Loki away and dispatched him.

As the last of the patrons moved into the gallery and Lily with them, Rowan moved around the corner, slipping through the door just as it fell closed. His eyes widened of their own accord as he looked around the room. Lily wasn't kidding; Loki had at least one of every weapon Rowan could name, and some he had never seen before.

More than once he caught Lily's gaze, followed immediately by a stern look from Loki, who less than thrilled with his presence, and incapable of doing anything about it. Rowan tried not to feel smug, but it didn't work. Despite the immediate danger, he enjoyed the hell out of the inconvenience his presence caused. It would work better if he could get to Lily, but he would be pushing his luck to try.

An irrational snarl of fury tangled in his gut as he glanced down at the case containing his father's journal. Writing he hadn't seen in more than three centuries until the previous night, the last link to his parents and his past, lay beneath inch-thick glass, in the possession of a thieving god.

As the crowd began to thin, leaving less and less distraction for Loki, Rowan slipped down the hallway and into the stairwell of the old building, Rowan stripped away his tuxedo, piece by piece. It would be a shame to destroy such a fine piece of tailoring, and while Dane might rake him across the coals for getting it dirty, at least it would still be in one piece. He shoved his clothes under the stairs, behind an old buffing machine, and took a moment to feel the cold air whispering around his ankles. The scents of food, perfume, and cigar smoke permeated the air, making it hard for him to pick out Loki's specific scent.

But Lily's...that was too easy. He would recognize that strawberry-and-summer scent across dimensions. Certain now that he'd been spotted, Loki would likely hang close to her, and Rowan knew he could use her scent to find him.

The crowd had come, eaten, and observed. Now it was down to the last few stragglers, the true history buffs that wanted to either argue the mythological origins, or the new-age nuts that whole-heartedly believed. Lily banished the train of thought before she could bash either side. She wasn't part of either crowd, yet she still wanted to dispute what she believed.

And Rowan…his presence in the room was both a blessing and a burden. With him there she felt safe, but she was drawn to him like a moth to the proverbial flame. Her gaze shifted to him over and over, but Loren's arm around her waist or his hand on her shoulder kept her rooted to the spot and his side.

Careful of your actions, he'd warned early in the night, and so far she had heeded that warning well. But Rowan slipped from view, and her heart fell. It was over. Rowan had failed. Loren still walked free, and with every second that passed, Lily grew closer to losing everything.

She had to get away from him, and had no idea how to do so. The safest bet was the storage room—claiming she needed cleaning supplies. Surely he wouldn't follow her there, and if he did, she would still have a valid reason for taking so long.

"I need to get ready for close-down," she whispered to Loki.

"I'll come with you."

Damn.

"Don't be silly," she sighed, trying to keep her voice light. "There are still patrons. One of us needs to be out here and I'm the one that's at work." Lily paused, then looked up at him, determined to play every card in her hand to get out if need be. "Besides, the storage room is nowhere near the door he just went through."

Loki didn't appear convinced, but he released his hold on her. Relief swept through her, and she pushed up on her toes to kiss his lips. The action surprised him; his eyebrows rose to his hairline.

"I'll be back in a minute," she promised, and swept from the room before he could respond. She breathed a rattling sigh of reprieve as the storage doors closed behind her. The cleaner and rags sat on one of the boxes, but she stuffed them under a series of discarded table covers to buy some time. If he did come looking for her, she could claim what she needed had been misplaced.

As expected, the door opened several moments later. Afraid to turn around, Lily busied herself by making a production of rifling through cabinets in search of her supplies.

"Are we alone in here?"

Lily froze, let that thick, rich voice pour over her. But...how had she not sensed him before? Simple. She was worrying, and trying not to pay attention to her surroundings.

"Lily, look at me." She paused, and slowly turned to face him. The sight of him was a welcome relief, and tears rushed to her eyes.

"Rowan...thank God," she breathed, and raced into his arms. The feel of his strong body against her broke open the flood gates. With tears streaming down her face, Lily dragged his face down and kissed him. In a moment of perfect happiness, their mouths met but it was...off. He tasted wrong. Maybe it was just stress, but it dawned on her as well that he wasn't as warm as usual. It was cold outside, she knew, but that had never seemed to matter before.

As the kiss drew to a close, she looked up at him. He was the same, except his eyes. Where she usually found passion and adoration, she found an odd lack of any emotion at all. The discovery tickled some buried thought that she couldn't quite recall. Then his gaze swept over her, and her heart kicked up a beat. "I've missed you," he said, voice low. He raised a hand to her face and drew his fingertips over her cheekbone. "I need you, Lily."

He lifted her from her feet and raised her to sit on a clear expanse of counter, stepping between her knees. His body pressed flush against hers, pushing her legs apart, and the slit in the side of her dress ripped almost to the hip. He didn't seem to notice.

"Rowan, this isn't safe," she protested as his lips descended on hers once more, silencing her argument. As his tongue swept over her bottom lip, though, she stopped caring. His mouth moved over hers, then to her cheek. He nipped at her ear, and licked a trail down her throat. When his fingers passed over the ring at her throat, it shivered.

She and Rowan both froze. He looked at it, then passed his finger over it again. The band shivered again, vibrating against her skin. She lifted it to her gaze, turning it over in her fingers. It was as if his touch had triggered some hidden catch; small runes danced along the inside of the band. She glanced up at him, and as recognition dawned in his features, realization sprouted in her mind. The speech pattern was wrong…the roughness of his touch… Oh, God…

This was not Rowan.

This was Loki.

He'd found the ring.

Lily pushed him backwards and shimmied off the counter. "I need to get back out there," she said, and went toward the spot where she'd stashed the cleaner.

"Maybe I should hold on to the ring…in case he sees it."

She hedged. "I'm okay."

"Lily," his voice held a warning. She could hear that now—the ice buried in his tone. The timbre was all wrong. She shivered.

"I promise, Rowan. Let me close up, okay?"

"Give me the ring."

"No."

"Why not?"

"Because you told me not to."

He hesitated. "Mistake," he said. "It's safer with me." Again, a manner of speaking that was wholly unlike Rowan. Lily quickly uncovered the cleaner and shifted toward the door, but her path was blocked.

Loki. As himself.

"Give me the ring, Lily."

She couldn't run. With no other option, as Loki advanced on her, she raised the bottle and sprayed the cleaner into his face. Even he was not fast enough to dodge the aerosol discharge completely. He shifted to one side, and clutched at his face, giving her the space she needed to throw open the door and run.

Lily made it as far as the gallery before the heel on her right shoe snapped and pitched her into the floor. She scrambled, tangled in her torn dress. She couldn't find her footing.

A feline snarl broke the silence, and looming over her as she looked up was a huge, jet-black panther. Lily took a deep breath, and praying Rowan was close enough to hear as Loki's four large paws stepped over her, pinning her to the floor, she screamed.

Bracing himself against the pain, Rowan pulled his power around himself like a cloak. Slivers of pain raced through his veins, twisting along muscle and bone as his body contorted and fur started to grow. Biting hard on his bottom lip to stifle the cry of agony associated with the shift, Rowan crouched toward the ground and let it take him.

When he stood again, he stood on four strong, solid paws. The cold no longer registered against his skin, and the draft caught his fur in a soft rustle. The animal instinct rose in the center of his brain.

Hunt.

Kill.

Protect his mate.

Rowan growled, a low snarl that echoed up the stairwell, and nosed open the door. On the other side of the wall, soft music still played. Somewhere near the back of the building, Lily screamed, but the sound came to an abrupt halt.

He sat back on his haunches, tipped his head to the ceiling, and howled. She was gone.

Lily closed her eyes and turned her face away. She knew her life was over, and yet her mind was strangely blank. Ignoring the wet puffs of breath on her cheek, she closed her hand around the ring and held tightly to it.

The low growl in his throat intensified, and a sickening sense of vertigo slipped over her. The world felt as if it were toppling over and over itself, loosening her hold on reality. The air shifted and the musty scent of the gallery was replaced with the clean, fresh scent of forest and water. Lily's eyes flew open, her heart racing, and in a rush of fur the panther's body flew across the room. His claws left a deep gouge in her shoulder, and the pain brought with it a wave of nausea that she fought hard to beat back.

The first thing she discovered was blistering pain. The second thing was the bright light of day. Clutching her torn shoulder she struggled into a sitting position as Loki, nude and in human form, came toward her from the edge of the tree line with the stained broadsword in his hand. They were outside. During the day. But this outside was nothing like she had ever seen before. The bright light around her carried a fine, blue-green hue. Everything seemed larger here, including Loki.

"W-where are we?" she asked, certain she didn't want to know the answer.

"Asgard," Loki replied. "Away from that meddling wolf."

"Why have you brought me here?"

"You have something I want."

"You aren't getting the ring."

"We are in my land, sweetheart," Loki said with a cruel laugh and stalked toward her. "There is little you can do to stop me here." Letting go of her shoulder, Lily closed her hand around the ring. Loki, unfazed, stabbed the sword into the ground and knelt before her, his hand extended.

"Give it to me."

"You're going to have to kill me," she said, sounding much braver than she felt.

"That can be arranged," he sneered and took hold of her wrist. Lily winced as he squeezed, popping the delicate bones with sudden, sharp pressure. She bit down hard on her lip to stifle her cry of pain, but she refused to let go of the small, gold band.

As her resolve started to crumble, Lily closed her eyes and took a shallow, shuddering breath. Her hold faltered, the band slipping between her fingers. The sharp jerk of the chain stung her skin but Loki dropped her arm, having gained his bounty.

A loud, banging crash echoed across the clearing, and Loki grunted. She lay there in the soft, dewy grass, cradling her ruined hand to her chest and listened to the sounds of battle. Someone yelped. And several heavy grunts issued forth. Lily turned toward the sound of the scuffle and forced her eyes open. A blur of tumbling fur and gnashing teeth greeted her. She could only discern the two by the colors of their pelts until Rowan caught Loki by the throat and flung him to the ground, bringing one large paw down against his head.

The wolf flew backwards, and Lily lost the fight again. Over and over Rowan was beaten back, bitten, raked. His strength was failing; she had to do something. Lily glanced around terrified. The sword stood in the ground next to her but she couldn't wield it one-handed. It was too big.

The exhausted yelp from Rowan kicked her into motion. He was pinned.

Fighting her own pain, Lily jerked the blade from the ground and dragged it toward the fight. She tried to raise it, but she was too weak.

And Loki saw her. He lunged for her and she rolled away, dropping the weapon. Screaming, she tried to flee, but his teeth sank into her already damaged shoulder. A weak gurgle echoed up her throat as he released her and swatted her.

She rolled away, the world a blur. Her side hit a stone buried in the grass, and shards of pain shot up and down her body. Then the pain stopped, replaced by a strange numbness and the floating feeling of timelessness. The world around her seemed to slow down into minute-long seconds. Everything appeared suspended in clear gel, taking effort to keep moving forward.

"Loki." The authoritative tone in Rowan's voice cut through the haze and she turned her head. Everything sped up again, the sudden burst of energy making her head spin. The panther poised above her, set to strike, turned its head toward him. She looked past Loki to Rowan standing across the clearing, human, naked, and holding Gram. The panther turned and lunged and the blade came down, severing its head from its shoulders with one clean sweep.

With that, the world went dark.

CHAPTER EIGHTEEN

Lily woke some time later to near silence. Her head ached, and for a moment she could not remember where she was. Recognition was slow as it returned. She remembered a fight. The panther. Rowan's voice. Then…nothing.

"Lily?"

Her eyes rolled around in her head, searching through the bright light until she found the source of the voice. Rowan floated above her, a disembodied face in the haze. She clung to his image; used it to pull herself back to reality. His arm was under her neck; his hand cradled her head. Every line of his face held worry.

"There you are," he said, relief flooding his voice.

"What's going on?" Her voice sounded ruined and rusty.

"I thought I had lost you." Lily tried to sit up as he spoke, but pain ripped through her side from her spine to her chest. Her mouth opened in a silent scream as the breath rushed from her lungs. "Hey, easy," he chided, and guided her curling body back to rest. "You were banged up pretty bad when he threw you. You might have broken a rib or two."

"Huh?" she gasped, still trying to both catch her breath and catch up.

"When Loki—" he started, and it all came rushing back. Despite the screaming agony throughout her body, she bolted upright, looking around.

"Oh, God," she whined as her eyes found the body across the glen, "he's…"

"Dead." After everything he'd said and done—all the lies, the threats, and the cruelty—Lily still felt tears puddle in the corners of her eyes. They threatened to spill down her cheeks as Rowan's arm closed around her, careful of her side. "I do not believe it," he said wondrously, tipping her face up. "After all the things he has done to you, you still want to weep for him."

"He wasn't all bad, Rowan…just selfish." She wiped a tear away before it had time to properly escape and blinked the rest away. "He was also attentive and generous."

"And a thief, Lily." Rowan's voice had gone cold and hard. Jealous.

"So are others, but we don't go around cutting their heads off."

He smiled, and traced her jaw with a fingertip. "You are so tenderhearted." He pulled her close and kissed her forehead. He smelled of sweat. Tiny drops of blood littered his skin, and that was when she realized he was still very much naked. She didn't have time to dwell on it though, because the sound of approaching footsteps echoed around them. She whimpered and fought against Rowan to get to her feet. He kept her down and still, and she quickly gave up the fight in favor of not moving to ease the pain.

She took a breath and clutched at her side as pain tore through it again. Pants of air came in short gasps as Rowan balanced her against his chest, and she whined as the sound of a cane thumping across the ground moved close and closer. She opened her mouth to speak, only to let loose a fountain of blood from her lips. Lily cast her horrified stare up at Rowan. "You're naked," she whispered, her strength failing. Hysteria rose as she once again located Loki's body, lying in a heap in the grass. Blood smeared the grass, the rocks, the sword, and their bodies. Her favorite dress was ruined.

"We need help," Rowan bellowed, rattling her eardrum and making her wince. She would have shied away from the sound, but a new, stabbing agony started in her side and nearly took her breath away.

"I am not here as a spectator," an old voice answered. Beside her, Rowan tensed as a man that very much matched the voice hobbled into view. His wild, white hair and beard drew her eyes, and in a moment of madness, she giggled and thought *he looks like Santa Claus!* The hysterical laughter quickly died as she took in the stark, black patch over one eye and the sad set to his grizzled, old jaw. He moved like a man exhausted with life, but not quite able to die. Something told her she should know who he was, but she couldn't quite place him. Then Rowan dropped to one knee, bowing his head as he pressed his right fist to his heart in salute, and Lily's breath caught in her throat.

"All-Father," Rowan said, his voice calm and reverent, confirming her sudden fear. *The Old God.* The old man responded in a language Lily did not understand. A niggling voice at the back of her mind told her she should fear this man for what power he did not show, but the exhaustion from the day's events was enough to wipe any sense of self-preservation from her mind.

When Rowan responded in the same foreign tongue, Lily gave up trying to understand anything at all and laid her head back against the ground with a thump.

"So it is done," Odin said. Rowan noted the hint of sadness in his voice, and could not stop the pang of guilt that ripped through him.

"Yes. The monster is slain." For one short moment, Rowan questioned his actions; wondered if the decision was just.

"I am sorry to hear of my brother's death," the old man replied, and Rowan cringed. "However, his actions were rash and your decision was justified." Rowan released a pent-up breath, and with it, centuries of frustration, determination, and agony. It was finally over. "To make an attempt on the life of one's mate is the worst crime. Worse even, I believe, than thievery, trickery, and the list of other crimes of which the old fool was guilty." A deep sigh rumbled from Odin. "I dare say this is my fault," he continued, and the admission surprised Rowan. "Had I not bade him make an excuse for the death of that boy, he would not have felt the need to steal the treasure. Granted," he chuckled softly, "Loki likely would have found a reason to go after it on his own, so I suppose my guilt is a bit silly." The old man thumped forward on his cane and laid a hand on top of Rowan's head. Rowan wasn't sure what he expected from the oldest of the gods, but a cold, human touch was not it. "Rise, my son."

Pride rippled through his chest as he stood. To have knelt in the presence of Odin the All-Father, to have been absolved of the death of an Old God, and to have risen as a son of Asgard...the burn of tears threatened his eyes.

"I must say," Odin said, and Rowan saw Lily's eyes widen—he realized that Odin had spoken in English, "your assessment of my dear brother is quite wrong, Rowan."

"Brother?" Lily squeaked, and the absolute truth that she wanted to avoid slammed into her. "You're..."

Odin.

"Yes, child," he confirmed. "I am afraid you have found me out." A coy smile danced around his lips, and he leaned heavily on the stick he carried. Rowan watched the exchange with great humor—he had tried to warn her about the existence of these beings, but she seemed to resolutely ignore everything he had to tell her...until now. She struggled to sit up as she listened. "I only ask that you do not hold poor Loki's greed against me. Sadly, this mess is all my doing. I thought him quite amusing at the time, but never did I imagine so many innocents would die for his selfish pride."

Rowan looked over at Lily again, and noticed that her skin was a bit paler than before, and a thin sheen of sweat had broken out across her forehead. "Are you all right?" he asked, and knelt to slip an arm around her shoulders. She turned to rubber in his grasp, but when he moved to pull her into his arms, she cried out in pain and collapsed back to the ground. He started to reach for her again, but a heavy hand came down on his wrist, stopping him.

"Let me." He hesitated, and turned his face toward the old man. "She is hurt far worse than you think."

Lily scarcely registered the exchange outside the crackling, electric pain in her side. When she tried to sit up something popped, and took the very breath out of her lungs. Her insides felt heavy and liquid, and it was all she could do to draw in each shallow breath around the pain. Even her heartbeat turned sluggish.

Heavy hands came down on her arm and her side and above her muffled voices argued. Lily couldn't understand them. She couldn't really understand anything but the pain, and even that was fading with every labored breath.

A slow, lingering warmth spread from those hands, reaching deep into muscle and bone. Lily was vaguely aware of shifting inside, and the recession of the heaviness, and then blissful dark. Voices were soft and distant, and though she was aware they were speaking of her, it didn't matter.

Loki was dead. Rowan was free. And Odin himself had just performed some sort of miracle on her. That was enough for one day.

Rowan had no idea what to do. All he could see was that Lily was hurt, dying even. In a moment of panic, he turned toward the old god before him and went down on his knees.

"Please, All-Father, what can I do to help her?"

The old man brushed his hands together and stood, leaning heavy on his staff. "She has three broken ribs. Her lung was punctured by one when she sat up, but that damage has been repaired. It could happen again." He fixed Rowan with a pointed stare. "She needs a healer. A mortal hospital."

His jaw worked like a broken hinge for a moment. "I cannot get her back on my own. My power is not that great."

"Take her up. We must make haste to Heimdall. He will send you home."

"That is all well and good, but…how do I explain the injuries?" Rowan asked as he lifted her limp body. Odin smiled down at him, his old eyes twinkling.

"Explain it for what it was. A panther attack."

"But I should not move her." He glanced around and cringed at the destruction. "How do I explain what happened?" Then it hit him. Just because he and Lily knew Loki was the same panther people had reported didn't mean everyone else in Savannah did. Odin chuckled.

"Glad to see that brain of yours still works, boy."

"But…there is no panther on the other side."

Odin glanced around as if confused, frowned, and lay his chin atop his hands, balanced on the staff. "So I see. Well, perhaps it is time to admit that Loki is not the only one prone to a bit of trickery." Again, his one visible eye sparkled with mischief. "I will not divulge all my secrets, but suffice it to say your panther problem will be quite solved by the time you get her into the hands of medical professionals."

Rowan did as he was told and stood, cradling the battered, whimpering girl to his chest. The old man started forward, pausing long enough to stand over Loki's dead form, sadness curling his lips down.

"My poor, foolish brother. Loki, you should have known better than to take that which was not yours." Then, chuckling as if proud of himself, Odin closed the distance between them and laid two fingers against Lily's forehead.

"Whatever you tell the human police, so will be her story too." He knelt and picked up the ring from the grass at Rowan's feet and, with it clasped in his hand stood and turned. "It is long past time for this to return to its rightful owner, don't you think?" Rowan nodded, a small bubble of panic rising at the sight of his ward in the hands of someone else. Odin laughed. "You worry too much, boy. Andvari and his children are long gone." He turned Rowan's palm up and laid the ring in it. "This little trinket has caused your family much trouble, and I am sorry to say it was my doing. The treasure and this ring were part of a payment made by Loki and me to your great-great grandfather for the death of his son." He closed Rowan's fingers around the cold, metal band. Bringing one hand down on his shoulder, Odin squeezed gently. "Keep this safe, and keep it in the family. You are free to live your life as you see fit now. I have done my part; the rest is up to you, my son. You have come this far... do not let me down now." Rowan felt something stir in his chest as Odin limped away, looking older and much more frail than he did when he entered the glade. There was only one thing left he wanted—no, needed—to do.

"All-Father, I have one more question."

He stopped and smiled. "The answer to that question has been right in front of you all along. You will find proof when you return to your world. Now turn north and make haste. Heimdall waits for you." And in a flash of light, Odin was gone. Rowan opened his hand and looked down at the gold band in his palm. So much trouble over such a little thing... so many years, and so many lives. He slipped it over the tip of his little finger—it was much too small to fit his hands properly—and limped forward, his right leg tender after his scuffle with Loki.

He broke through the tree line as Lily's whimpers and cries turned to low, gurgling groans. A thin line of blood trickled from her lips toward her shoulder. Frightened by the sight, Rowan picked up his pace, running toward the white marble pedestal where the bifrost stood, a gleaming gold-and-stone portal guarded by the tall man with the ivory horn. Heimdall nodded and lifted the horn to his lips as Rowan approached, and as the low, melancholy sound echoed around them the portal opened, allowing access back to Midgard, and more specifically, Savannah, Georgia.

"Thank you," Rowan said as he darted into the swirling vortex. His grip on Lily tightened as his sense of balance pitched forward and spit him into the center of the ruined art gallery. He laid Lily carefully on the ground and pulled back the shredded scraps of her dress, but before he could properly assess her injuries paramedics pushed him to the side. He stepped back, glancing sidelong at the dead panther lying inside the foyer, then turned and paced in circles. At some point, Odin had seen fit to give him clothes—he did not remember putting them on and suspected he hadn't. As the emergency team loaded Lily onto a stretcher, he paced over to the one remaining upright case. Lying atop a stand, untouched except for the litter of glass fragments in its spine, was his father's book. Scrawled in his father's hand across the tattered old page were the three words he'd hoped to find all along.

The Mating Ritual

Rowan breathed a sigh of relief and glanced over at Lily injured and being wheeled toward the waiting ambulance, but alive and free. The police officer with the notebook approached, prepared to ask questions of Rowan, but he didn't mind. All he cared about was that Lily was going to be all right.

And when she was well again, he would make her his.

EPILOGUE

Eight weeks later…

Lily glanced down at the cold, golden band around her left ring finger. She'd nearly died trying to protect the damn thing, so it seemed a fitting way to end its journey, but still…why the hell was she so nervous? She'd already slept with Rowan a dozen or more times. She'd been attacked by a god, saved by another, and grilled by the police about some wild panther attack that she knew wasn't the truth, yet had no problem at all lying about. True, she still had moments of panic when she thought Loki would come back to get her — after all, he'd escaped death so many times before. So why exactly was her stomach in knots over this one little ceremony?

Because her life was changing.

Lily's mother fussed over her, twirling her curls just so, fluffing the hem of her gown in preparation for the pictures that she so dreaded. When she'd called her mother to tell her the happy news (*"Mom, I'm getting married!"*), she hadn't expected quite this reaction. Donna Redway had jumped on the first plane back to Savannah, practically levitated as she welcomed Rowan into the family, and then spent the next three weeks shamelessly spending Rowan's money on the wedding of the century.

"Mom, that's enough," Lily ordered, to no avail. Her mother snorted and continued her duties.

"Mrs. Redway," Rowan cooed, "Lily is beautiful no matter how you organize her hair. She is your masterpiece, and she is perfect just the way she is." The older woman visibly swooned, and Lily rolled her eyes. She'd heard the ancient and sometimes archaic flattery so much that she had grown immune to it. Her mother, however was still prone to his genteel, masculine wiles. With a groan, Lily elbowed Rowan in the ribs, and was rewarded with a muffled oof for her trouble.

"Suck-up," she whispered as the photographer herded them into place. He smiled and kissed her forehead.

With the wedding and reception done, Rowan swept her up and all but ran up the stairs in his house, his lips dancing along her jaw and throat with each step. A deep rumble echoed out of his chest, and Lily's heart beat out a hard, unsteady rhythm.

She'd married him. What was the big deal?

The big deal was the raw power coursing through and around him. The air shimmered just as it had when she watched him shift. A small kernel of terror rose in her throat at the thought of his beastly nature, but it was a little late for that.

No, what frightened her more than anything was the way that power reached out for her, called to her, pulled her in. It wanted her because he wanted her. Because she had agreed to marry him, to be his mate. To be bound to him forever.

"You realize you got off way too easy, right?" Lily asked as he ascended the stairs. Rowan's chest rumbled with laughter.

"What do you mean?"

"You tricked me."

He stopped. His face turned serious, and his arms started to shiver. Lily feared for a moment he might drop her. "How so?"

"Well," she said, her voice thin and reedy, "you promised me a job, instead you almost got me killed."

Rowan roared with laughter and pushed into the bedroom. Gently, he placed her on the bed, careful of both her still tender ribs and her dress—all of it, she thought with a groan—and tipped her face up to his.

"I did not almost get you killed. Your stubborn pride did that."

"But you could have been honest."

"I tried, but you refused to let me, remember?" He smiled at her. "If you really feel that way..." He stood and moved like he would leave the room. Lily grabbed his arm and pulled him back.

"No," she said a little too fast, "but I am going to hold it against you for a long time."

"Oh, I hope you do. I hope you hold everything against me." Lily snorted and swatted at him.

"You're such a goofball. That's not what I mean."

"Oh, then by all means, please elaborate."

"You owe me, big boy."

"So you want me to grovel?" he asked, going down on one knee with a wicked smile.

"For starters."

"And beg your forgiveness?"

Lily chewed the inside of her cheek to keep from laughing. She looked away, hoping he took it as frustration and not a means of keeping her humor at bay. "That's more like it," she said, forcing her voice to stay even.

"Then let me try this," he said, and turned her face back to his. His demeanor was still and serious, and his pale eyes shone with love. "Lily Keir," he said, voice no louder than a whisper. She shivered at her new name. "You have agreed to become my mate. Do you understand the responsibility that comes with such an agreement?"

She had the momentary thought that she should tell him this was silly, but she couldn't. This was serious, the way of his people. She could give him everything he wanted, and exactly the way it needed to happen. She let her smile unfurl as she met his steady gaze.

"I do."

"Do you give yourself willingly to me, mind, body, and soul?" he asked.

"I do." Again she felt the brush of power along her skin, a crackling, electric current that tugged at her senses.

"I give to you of myself everything I have. Mind, body, and soul. Do you accept me?"

"I do." The swirl of energy grew stronger around her. The hairs on her arms and across the back of her neck stood on end. He took hold of her, his big hands clasped around her wrists. Instinct took over. She turned her hands and held his arms in the same fashion. "Do you accept me?"

He smiled. "I do."

"Then make me your mate."

A thin, weak groan issued from his throat as he pulled her into his arms and kissed her. Lily slid her arms around his neck and pulled him to her, lying backwards. His weight came down on her, and whatever this power was surrounding them closed in, enveloping them in each other. With each touch of his hand or brush of his lips, the bond between them grew stronger, turned into something tangible. And as he entered her, their souls bonded, twining together into one being. For a moment time stretched out before her, and she knew, as she did the moment she laid eyes on him, that he was the one. His fingers threaded through hers and clasped her hand, using it as leverage when he moved over her. She cried out in pleasure and the fear of this commitment dissipated, leaving only glowing warmth in her chest and a feeling of euphoria coursing through her body.

Together they cried out, a single voice of release, and as he rolled to his side and gathered her into his arms, she could feel him nestled safely in her heart. Her husband. Her mate.

"Lily?"

"Yes, Rowan?"

"I love you."

"I love you, too."

"Forever?"

Lily sighed and curled into his side. She lay her cheek against his chest and listened to the strong sound of his heartbeat. She could never remember being happier. "Forever."

ACKNOWLEDGEMENTS

Thank you to everyone who has stuck with me all these years. I have some truly amazing friends and family and I couldn't possibly have come this far without any of them. My mother, my husband... they've been beside me, cheering me on all this time. My friends — the *Shenanigators* ladies in particular — have kept me sane, talked me down, and generally been the most amazing support system in the world. I love every single one of them more than I can express with words alone.

And then there are my readers. All of you crazy, wonderful people who keep coming back...from the bottom of my black, little heart, thank you. I appreciate every single one of you.

ABOUT THE AUTHOR

Siobhan originally started out as a Dungeons & Dragons character.

True story.

She was an obnoxious little blonde-haired, violet-eyed half-elf rogue who had a bad habit of screaming at random and stealing things from her fellow travelers. She was chaotic neutral, so it pretty much meant she never had to say she was sorry.

She made the transition from fantasy RPG character to fantasy literary character in 2011. S.H. Roddey wrote a story out of her usual genre, and she decided she needed a pen name rather than confuse her audience. Naturally, Siobhan stepped up and said she'd take the blame. Since then, Siobhan has learned to be a little less of a kamikaze even if she never grew out of being a walking calamity.

The romance is strong with this one. Some is sweet and some is spicy. It's about half and half on the paranormal/contemporary fields, and all of it is quite good Of course, if you were to ask Siobhan, she'd likely tell you that her creator didn't have a thing to do with it.

Oh, and for those who aren't sure, it's pronounced *Shi-von*.

FIND SIOBHAN ONLINE

Blog
http://siobhankinkade.wordpress.com

Facebook
https://www.facebook.com/AuthorSiobhanKinkade

Twitter
https://www.twitter.com/SiobhanKinkade

Monthly Newsletter
https://landing.mailerlite.com/webforms/
landing/j4o5o7

Facebook Group
https://www.facebook.com/groups/2181499065248034/

ALSO BY SIOBHAN KINKADE

PARANORMAL ROMANCE
Marked
She-Wolf
Blood Doll

PARANORMAL ROMANCE
Something in the Air
Letting Go
Homegrown Hearts

FROM MOCHA MEMOIRS PRESS
Huntress
Under the Mistletoe

FROM PURPLE SWORD PUBLICATIONS
Frozen Hearts & Blazing Souls

Printed in the USA
CPSIA information can be obtained
at www.ICGtesting.com
LVHW042203011224
798080LV00033B/697

* 9 7 9 8 6 6 5 9 8 3 6 8 4 *